THE WORM AND HIS KINGS

HAILEY PIPER

Manuscript copyright 2020 Hailey Piper
Logo copyright 2020 Off Limits Press
Cover photo copyright 2020 by Filip Dinev
Cover design by Squidbar Designs
Interior design by Squidbar Designs
Edited by Karmen Wells

"The space circumvented by wormholes can only be a worm."

– Corene Valencia, professor in physics at Queens College,
City University of New York

1

THE EMPTY PLACE

MONIQUE LANE HAD PROMISED HERSELF she would never return to Freedom Tunnel. Yet here she was, two weeks later, promise broken.

Freedom Tunnel had been a line for freight trains until its shutdown in 1980, and in 1990 it remained in official disuse. No trains passed through anymore; only people, and some of them built homes here. If there were any justice in Manhattan, the tunnel would stay this way and leave all its residents be, but Monique knew better than to expect justice in this town. At a distance, it might have seemed little different from any other underground railroad. Tracks slipped inside, inviting ghost trains into premature dusk.

But closer to the entrance, she hesitated, same as she had every evening when she lived here. Was there nowhere else to go? The city's alleys were unkind, but at least there she feared things that she could touch and see.

Freedom Tunnel's floor was level, like much of Manhattan, and yet looking into the concrete mouth, its throat always seemed to dip toward the bowels of the Earth. No one but

Monique seemed to know about the empty place inside, or if others did, they never talked about it. No grown adult would out themselves as fearing a dreadful nothing in the dark.

Often she hugged her empty stomach and cried outside the tunnel, among beer bottles and scattered plastic bags. No heading inside until she was done. She never wanted the empty place to hear. No one could touch that emptiness, but noises had to travel through it. Sometimes people sang to themselves in the dark, Broadway tunes or Dolly Parton songs, and Monique would've sung along but for fear that the empty place might catch those notes in its nothingness.

The same went for crying. Better not to have her misery's echoes trapped and wriggling in its web.

Long-buried phantoms seemed to wander the subterranean twilight. Only when Monique's eyes adjusted did scant light reveal those phantoms to be ordinary people. ConEd sometimes powered the lights here, sometimes didn't, though residents often pirated electricity off the main line either way.

Some chose to be here; others had nowhere else. There was space to spare and yet most, especially those who had built firm structures of wood or piled cinder blocks, chose the same places to rest every time they returned. Freedom Tunnel was home.

No one had touched Monique's makeshift tent of weathered blankets fastened to rusty wall rivets. Though everyday residents likely knew she hadn't been back in several nights, they must have heard she was still out in the city, spending half of each day begging for change and the other half asking after Donna Ashton. She hadn't gone missing like Donna and a few dozen other homeless people. Freedom Tunnel had been waiting and remained unchanged.

The empty place hadn't changed either.

Beside Monique's tent lay a stretch of floor where no one slept. She had almost set her things there when she first arrived but thought better of it and set up along the wall to its left instead. Some days, she watched others do the same. They approached with sleeping bags, old coats, or nothing at all, looking for a place to belong in this steel and concrete neighborhood. Then without warning, they changed their minds and found another spot in the dark. The empty place was cleaner than the rest of Freedom Tunnel, too. Not even dust would settle there.

It made Monique's skin crawl and put a chill in her bones. Each time she reached out to touch that bare stretch of floor, thinking to dispel the mystique, she withdrew her hand within an inch. "You're just being silly," she would mutter to herself.

But then a minute would pass, or an evening, and the empty sense of it would creep back across her mind. Sometimes a face formed in the gloom, both new and yet seen in a thousand glances. He'd have nothing to say, but he would grin at her and start for the empty place as if to sit beside her. Within a few steps, his expression would slacken, and he'd decide there were better places to rest. Even creeps feared the empty place.

At least creeps were a tangible threat, reason for Monique to fasten belt leather around her bicep, which held a switchblade up her sleeve while she slept. No knife would threaten the empty place. She felt its nothingness in the dark some nights when the electricity faltered and kerosene lamps and burn barrels cast dancing shadows across graffiti-coated walls. And in her sleep, it sent cold shapes clawing at her dreams.

Tonight, she wouldn't sleep. She'd chosen to come back here not because of the troubles in alleys or to torture herself with the empty place beside her tent. She'd come back for Donna.

The empty place made Monique feel like she was losing her mind, but rumor had it there was a genuine flesh-and-blood nightmare stalking the city. Street folk were going missing, all of them women, without a word to neighbors and friends, and they left their things behind. At least one vanished each night, going back three months from what anyone knew.

There was nothing in the newspapers far as Monique ever noticed, the rumors passing person to person. This city liked to forget people. No surprise that some of those stories had taken on a mythic tone. Some liked to joke about the Jersey Devil or that Cropsey had wandered over from Staten Island. Others didn't joke when they said a monster they'd dubbed Gray Hill had been frequenting Freedom Tunnel of late. There were only ever a couple hundred people living here, most too stubborn to leave. It might've been no more than a street-spawned boogeyman, but like alligators in the sewers, there was no telling just how real anything might be in New York City. Women living rough were disappearing and something was taking them.

The same might have happened to Donna. She had been missing for three months; who was to say she hadn't been the first? That would explain why she hadn't left a trace.

Only her hope of finding Donna could drag Monique back to Freedom Tunnel. She had to see Gray Hill for herself.

She hadn't left any clothes in the tent, already wearing most of what she owned. Tufts of black hair spilled past her cherry red beanie, down round cheeks, and over the scarves that encircled her neck. An oversized black T-shirt hung loose across her ribs. Her denim jacket covered the scratches down her arms, while jeans hid the scars that ran along one side of her abdomen and between her thighs.

The thin blanket she'd left behind smelled of herself and others who might've squatted in her tent during her absence. She wished it smelled like Donna. A scent undefinable and yet uniquely hers, it made Monique think of their old apartment, the walks they used to take, the shelter where they'd stayed after this past winter's ordeal, and Donna tending to Monique's bandages there.

Donna smelled like home. Of course her scent wasn't here. She'd vanished before Monique had found Freedom Tunnel, and any sense of home here was an illusion. Railways were transitory. At some point, passengers had to reach journey's end.

Maybe it was at last time to return to Flushing. Monique had spent the last year and a half dodging her parents' neighborhood. She half-expected that if she were to visit, she would find an empty lot where she once lived, her mother and father having fled to Brooklyn or maybe northern Jersey with their house impossibly in tow.

Really, if she showed up begging for a place to sleep, they might take her. But she would have to live the life they wanted for her and promise to never again humiliate them with peculiarities, like having thoughts and opinions of her own. Their self-assuredness wouldn't have shriveled. If she turned up on their doorstep with Doctor Sam's scars running down her body and her bones pressing from beneath starving skin, that

4

would only feed their pride.

There was no going back. Between her parents' house and the street, it was only a matter of lasting as long as she could in a place that would slowly kill her.

She ran her hand down her face and hesitated, palm clutching mouth and nose shut. She could hold it there until her air ran out. That would be life every day if she went back to her parents, dying alone at the ripe old age of twenty.

Her hand dropped to her chest. "Not a quitter," she whispered. Pride might have been hereditary. She curled one hand into a loose fist and rapped her knuckles against her sternum.

Donna used to do that to her. "I like your chest this way," she'd said while they laid on the couch in their old apartment, after Monique had complained about her shape. Donna had then tapped out a rhythm. "Shave and a haircut—" Monique had pushed her gently, pretending to be annoyed, but Donna wouldn't let up. "Great for telling knock-knock jokes, silly Mon Amour." Not that she'd known any good ones, but she never let that stop her. "Knock, knock."

Monique tapped her chest again, but it wasn't the same when alone in Freedom Tunnel. The empty place clawed at her thoughts and tore them from sweet reminiscence. Its touch would taint those memories if she gave it the chance, turn love into resentment.

But she couldn't help that. Donna had promised to keep the two of them from places like Freedom Tunnel. And if she couldn't keep that promise, they should've slept together in this ragged tent. Being alone in this place was not what love felt like. Donna was older, more worldly, and should've been here to hold Monique's hand, stroke her hair, and guard her from the empty place. On the nights when Monique woke up panicked by ugly nightmares—desperate people drowning in concrete beneath the blankets, grasping at her, pulling her down—Donna should've said, *That's just the tunnel haunting your dreams, Mon Amour. It's okay to sleep.*

Deep down, Monique didn't need Donna to tell her they were only nightmares. Same as there was no one beside her, there was no one beneath Freedom Tunnel. This was rock bottom; nowhere deeper to go. But still, she would've slept easier with Donna's precious whispers in her ear.

As lights dimmed down the tracks, Monique reached past

the edge of her makeshift tent's flap, fingers searching for Donna. Maybe the darkness would spit her up and back into Monique's life.

Only the empty place lay beside her. There was no hand to hold.

Rough, heavy cloth scraped the tunnel's throat. Freedom Tunnel ran three miles long, and something now walked its central tracks, the footsteps going *click, click* against hard concrete. For all Monique knew, albino reptilian jaws swam the darkness, ready to bring sharp white death.

The empty place dragged cold fingers across her spine. She reached into her sleeve and fingered her switchblade's trigger, but there was nothing to fight. The empty place was just restless. *This is why the likes of you can't set foot here*, it might have said. *I'm a table for one, reserved by a monster.* And now a monster was coming.

The air turned static, every tunnel resident rousing to a collective awareness. Some of them shuffled in the dark to leave, but most stayed put. Either they didn't believe in Gray Hill or, like Monique, they wanted to see.

She poked her head out of the tent. Few lights dotted the tunnel this late at night and none spread their luminance far, leaving the walls and floor painted black between secluded camps. No light at all touched Freedom Tunnel's throat. Whatever walked there walked unseen.

Monique pressed flat to the ground, her eyes fixed open. If she even blinked, she might wake up. Much as she would've liked to pretend this wasn't real, she needed to see.

The shape filled the night. Bulky hips suggested a woman, but her overall shape was hard to discern, the way heavy cloth draped her arms, legs, and back. The suggestion of a hooded head climbed ten feet off the ground. Her spine hunched forward, suggesting that her head could rise higher if Gray Hill ever stood up straight.

"Ooh?" she called. A deep, throaty question, like a whale's song trapped underground.

There was more shuffling in the tunnel now of frightened onlookers regretting that they'd stayed.

Gray Hill took another step and sank into a pool of darkness. Her footsteps thudded closer, her body veiled in shadow. She emerged a few feet from Monique, a nearby kerosene lamp painting the outline of a billowing cloak. Firelight reflected in silvery talons on Gray Hill's hands and feet. Her legs bent backward, birdlike, and one toe of each foot curled upward into a vicious sickle claw.

Monique clamped a hand back over her nose and mouth. Maybe this thing had taken Donna and would lead the way to her, but Monique didn't mean to be taken herself. Returning here was a mistake. Freedom Tunnel invited impossible things.

Gray Hill waded through night's black river, disappearing from all of Freedom Tunnel's light. Where was she? *Click, click*, the sound of talons against concrete stepped past Monique and toward islands of light.

"Ooh!" A foghorn blasted up the tunnel. Shadowy arms tore into one tent and knocked away its burn barrel. Embers spit along the tunnel tracks, dousing all sight of Gray Hill just as she grabbed a woman off the ground. Someone was shrieking, but Monique couldn't tell if that was the woman in the monster's hand or a neighbor who just wanted this nightmare to end.

Talons scraped closer, closer, and then past Monique. Heavy cloth brushed the tent's edge and tumbled across her head. Its fabric felt rough, like burlap. Her breath ran hard against her hand.

Gray Hill's clicking footsteps paused just past the tent. A distant kerosene lamp cast a silhouette of her bent spine. She aimed her head at Monique. No one screamed now. Whoever Gray Hill held didn't even whimper, as if all her air had been squeezed out. Firelight reflected in a puffy red coat. Monique's red beanie might've been just as easy to see.

She wanted to close her eyes, but now they wouldn't blink. If she blinked, those talons would take her.

Thick breath whipped the makeshift tent around her. One stiff blow from those enormous arms would sweep the blankets away, but Gray Hill didn't move. Did she do this each night when she came to Freedom Tunnel? No, because Monique hadn't been here the other nights. Someone would've risked a photo had Gray Hill lingered this long every time.

Monique felt a chill then, as if someone her size had slipped inside the tent and now pressed against her, their body cold as ice, but there was no one with her. She eyed the monster again and realized she'd misunderstood.

Gray Hill wasn't looking at the tent. She was looking at the empty place.

It couldn't be coincidence. For all the people Monique had seen sidestep that bare stretch of Freedom Tunnel, this monster was the only creature besides herself to pay unwavering attention to it. Gray Hill felt the empty place's nothingness, and one nightmare acknowledged another, kin calling kin. A faint cry crawled up from Monique's guts. She clenched her mouth shut. Which nightmare would notice her first and tear her apart?

One sickle-clawed foot slid toward Freedom Tunnel's throat, and then the *click, click* resumed. The empty place had stalled Gray Hill long enough. She had what she needed and was headed back the way she'd come. Darkness took her completely. Her heavy footsteps faded, and for a moment the tunnel was silent.

Monique exhaled hard. At first she held still like that, forgetting how to inhale. Then whispers filled the tunnel. She couldn't make out their words, but their presence told her it was okay to breathe, so she took a deep breath. Eventually she would stop thinking about breathing and it would become natural again.

She clambered to her feet, stepped toward the rails, and faced Freedom Tunnel's pitch-black throat. There was nothing to see. The quiet tunnel acted as if there had been no creature, that the darkness itself had snatched that poor woman. She might be dead already. Monique hoped not, both for the woman's sake, and because there was a good chance that one of these nights, that darkness had snatched Donna.

No one stood outside her tent now that Gray Hill was gone. There never would be anyone so long as Monique stayed here. These past three months had brought nothing but empty hands and an empty stomach.

What were her choices now? Give up, accept nothing? She had fought too long to quit. If she followed Gray Hill, there was at least a chance to find Donna. She was out there somewhere. Even if this thing had killed her, Monique needed to know.

There was nothing to pack. If she couldn't find Donna at

the end of this, either that thing would kill her, or she'd finally starve to death on the streets. A nothing life with a nothing end.

Her gaze drifted again to the empty place. Nothing was all she would leave behind.

2
DOWN FREEDOM'S THROAT

GRAY HILL DID NOT TAKE her time. Though the tunnel went pitch-black at points, she seemed to find her way down tracks and around steel columns with ease. Now and then, her head crested beneath a ceiling grate, where ghostly light trickled from Manhattan's busy nightlife.

Monique hadn't eaten in two days, but she'd scrounged enough change for a quart of milk yesterday, which had tricked her stomach into thinking it was full, and she'd kept herself hydrated today. She could manage the tunnel's three miles.

Pace was another story. Gray Hill had long limbs that let her sweep briskly down the tracks. Monique bounded with each step, trying to time her footfalls with Gray Hill's, but it took more effort to keep human legs in stride. Soon their underground world would join the city's cacophony of traffic, music, and rumbling subway, and then Monique would have no excuse not to run.

It would be her fault if Gray Hill got away.

Freedom Tunnel's mouth was clean by comparison to its throat. Though garbage drifted outside, frequent foot traffic through the shantytown kept dust from settling too much, and what rust corroded the rails made it feel lived-in rather than decaying. Since the freight line's shutdown, the rest of the tunnel had become a largely untraveled stretch of underground, and the rails wore dust like a skin. Doubtful that those who disappeared would ever be found.

Monique would be the same if caught.

She'd wondered over the past three months if Donna might have vanished on purpose, resentful over losing her position at the law offices of Marigold & Cohen. Her colleagues' discovery of her relationship with Monique had murdered all aspirations for becoming a partner someday, years of hard work down the gutter. Donna had every right to throw blame wherever she pleased.

Yet she never did. "It's for the best," she'd said, almost chipper when they'd carried two cardboard boxes out the lobby doors. "Thirteen years and I never found my purpose here. Maybe now, I will."

She hadn't found it in her nice apartment either. Without the high-end job, she eventually couldn't afford high-end rent and had to move into Monique's tiny Brooklyn apartment. A poor choice since Monique didn't have the best track record with homes. A rent hike soon put her, Donna, and twenty other tenants on the street. The pizza place where Monique worked then closed down. Life was a series of shutting doors, their outsides knob-free, the buildings themselves packing up and running away from her fast as they could.

Monique had speculated that Donna was the same and couldn't blame her. But now there was this creature.

Gray Hill slowed ahead, forcing Monique to squirm back into the shadows. There wasn't much noise from the street above, but they were under River Side; there would be hustle and bustle soon. A narrow ceiling grate cast faint light across Gray Hill's hand, where a silhouette of limp limbs dangled between lengthy fingers. The unconscious woman's red coat could easily swap for a red beanie if Monique wasn't careful.

Gray Hill swerved from the tracks toward a shadow-covered wall. A scraping sound filled the tunnel, like cloth being rubbed across a rough surface.

11

Monique watched the darkness, urging her eyes to adjust.

Gray Hill was shrinking. Layers of cloth squeezed against her gargantuan yet narrow limbs and folded her into a fissure in Freedom Tunnel's wall. Graffiti whispered chartreuse letters to either side. Hopefully the artist had foregone exploring this slender opening, or else Monique expected to step over a derelict can of spray paint.

She waited a minute after the wall had swallowed Gray Hill and then ran up to the crevice. Concrete teeth rubbed her palms as she felt at the edges, but they didn't chomp down. She slipped inside.

Rough scraping led her through the black passage. She took careful steps not to kick up debris. Gray Hill was doing plenty of that herself as she squeezed along, building a thick dust cloud in her wake. Monique pulled a scarf over her mouth not to breathe it in. One cough, and the jig was up. She felt at the cold plastic handle up her left sleeve, but against a monster with hands the size of manhole covers, her switchblade was little better than a security blanket.

Her only advantage was the passage's narrowness. While Gray Hill had to shimmy forward in uncomfortable bursts, Monique walked free. Keeping up became easy.

Faint light soon cut Gray Hill's ten-foot silhouette from the blackness. She made one more forceful push and then snapped loose from the passageway. Her captive's red coat shimmered to life just as she veered left.

Monique crept toward the jagged exit, waited to be sure Gray Hill had kept moving—sounded like it—and then poked her head out.

A subway tunnel opened to the right and left. Rainbows of graffiti colored the concrete walls between small round lights. Their glow reflected in the tunnel's steel tracks. These weren't the harmless freight rails of Freedom Tunnel; a third rail spit electricity up and down the subway line between Monique and the far wall. One wrong step and the chase would end in merciless lightning.

Though only wide enough for single-tracking, the subway tunnel was spacious compared to the narrow path within the walls. Gray Hill walked in stride here and would soon leave Monique in the dust.

The third rail taunted. Monique could almost hear its hum.

It wasn't high, easy to step over as any other track, but she couldn't trust it not to reach for her when she tried. This city had been trying to kill her for the longest time. She followed along a ways with an eye on her gray prize.

If she couldn't handle crossing the third rail, how would she handle Gray Hill once they reached her lair? Monique tensed her body and took a breath. One shoe scraped across concrete. She rushed forward and jumped.

Both shoes landed on the far side of the third rail without touching it. The city would have to try to kill her another day.

"Ooh?" Gray Hill croaked something between a guttural frog's call and a deep whale song.

It echoed down the subway tunnel and through Monique's nerves. She dropped flat on her stomach. Her hands splayed, and her arms knotted against the concrete floor in case she needed to bounce up and run. Her only chance then would be the passage back to Freedom Tunnel. Out in the subway, Gray Hill could grab her with a free hand and squeeze until every bone snapped and organ popped, leaving a puddle for transit workers to find with a red beanie sitting like a cherry on top of melted ice cream.

Monique shook the idea away; terror would only make her make mistakes. She had to hold still and pretend she wasn't here, not imagine what Gray Hill would do if she found her. Imagination always got the best of people. Monique blamed Doctor Sam for the steady strain of paranoia she'd been living with since this past winter, when last she and Donna faced a monster.

By the time life put them on the street, they had already met Samuel Reinhart, good old Doctor Sam, and paid him in advance to operate on Monique. They couldn't get the money back after their eviction. Even living rough, it only made sense to go ahead with his sketchy surgery.

Monique blamed herself for not seeing through his promises and smiles. He would've taken their money and run, leaving them confused and heartbroken in a gray city snowbank, had he not planned to pull greater riches from beneath her skin and muscle.

Donna had been wary of him from the start. If not for her, Monique wouldn't still be walking with two kidneys. She was unconscious when the good doctor showed his true colors and only heard scant details later from Donna over how they got out of there, events involving a scalpel and teeth. Doctor Sam didn't bear Monique's scars, but he hadn't walked away entirely unscathed.

That was all Donna's doing. Monique would not be useless this time, and she wasn't going to quit, no matter the silvery talons or sickle claws.

Click, click. Gray Hill was on the move. She had to suspect she wasn't alone here. With every heavy footstep, the chance to find Donna slipped farther away.

Monique hopped to her feet and darted up the tracks. No, no, Gray Hill couldn't escape now.

The tunnel curved. Ahead and to the right, concrete walls first gave way to steel columns and then to an open platform. Light spilled from its ceiling, casting commuter shadows across the tracks. Within minutes, a train would come plowing from the darkness, its horn warning everyone to keep the hell out of its way.

At the light's edge, Gray Hill reached for the ceiling and popped open a rectangular grate. She placed her unconscious prisoner inside and then dragged herself up the wall and into the ceiling. The opening seemed narrow, but her clothing squeezed against her body, almost like a bird's feathers, and she made it through. For all Monique knew, plumage might have hidden beneath those billowing clothes.

The grate clanged shut, and Gray Hill disappeared. Whether that grate led to another layer of the underground or a discreet alleyway, she was getting away.

Monique dashed for the platform. An unseen busker sang "Fortunate Son" in a grizzled voice, fighting commuter chatter and rumbling subway cars for attention. Monique hoped the crowd would be too focused on themselves to notice her scrabbling at the platform's corner. If there was a ladder to make climbing up easier, she didn't see it, but she managed to climb up. She took a second to breathe and then took off, her weary limbs complaining. Her body didn't understand that Gray Hill wouldn't wait up.

Behind scattered commuters, a parallel set of tracks welcomed a screeching train. Its arrival blew hot wind and paper debris at Monique's face. The commuters who slipped out its doors next funneled toward ascending concrete stairs.

Monique followed them to another underground subway level, where she slid past a row of turnstiles and began to push through a thickening crowd.

Commuters waiting in line at the ticket booth glanced or stared at her. She was used to being a shadow creature, but now she was in a hurry and making onlookers curious. They might report her to a transit worker if they thought she'd hopped the turnstiles or picked a pocket. Serious trouble or not, any delay would help Gray Hill vanish into the night.

Monique slowed beside one man who wore a suit and tie. "Spare change?" she asked. "Every bit helps."

He slapped the pockets of his designer pants in an exaggerated gesture and gave a wan smile. "Sorry, nothing on me," he said, and hurried toward a magazine stand.

She slapped her thighs too. "Me neither." She didn't believe him—men who dressed like that counted every penny when they bought their morning coffee—but she didn't mind for once. No one looked at her now, lest she ask them for a nickel next. Invisible again, she hurried up the next stunted flight of steps.

She emerged at an intersection. Orderly streetlights dotted the sidewalks; pedestrians stepped briskly beneath them and crossed the streets wherever they pleased. Gray office buildings and brickwork apartments formed lines down each block. Colorful lights dotted windows to mark a deli or corner store. Adjacent from the subway exit stood Empire Music Hall, an elegant Greek revival of white columns and dark glass. It seemed like the one place that wasn't selling something, but only because it was closed for the evening.

No sign of Gray Hill. Two subway grates broke up the sidewalk nearby, but that didn't mean she had climbed through either of them.

Monique darted along dark windows, her beanie's reflection becoming a grim red blur. That monster was her one lead, and even then it was a long shot. Now Gray Hill was gone. She would have heard a noisy leap in the subway and wouldn't be so careless next time. She could pop up in Central Park, Morningside Park, grab someone off any Harlem subway platform, maybe venture farther south, and abandon Freedom Tunnel for all time. Monique might never find her again.

She should've tried to get the monster's attention beside the empty place and let herself be snatched. Now she'd lost Donna. Forever.

"Ooh."

The sound might've been a busted car horn, but Monique didn't think so. The chase wasn't over yet. She darted across Morningside Avenue toward the foot of Empire Music Hall's broad steps, where its white columns towered skyward. From the top, she'd have a decent vantage point.

"Ooh." The sound came more muffled this time, as if still underground. Monique almost felt it through her feet as she crested the steps. She was close.

Her heart banged a snare drum rhythm as she reached the top step, where a corpse waited for her behind the black glass double doors. It stood on two legs, moving in synch with her steps and pausing when she paused.

Her heart settled and she felt ridiculous. That was no walking corpse; it was only her reflection. No one stood behind Empire Music Hall's double doors.

Yet her reflection didn't look like she did right now, wide-eyed and panting and shaking. It looked dead, its gaze hollow, its skin chalky. She tried not to stare, but her eyes wouldn't turn away. It put the thought in her head that if she stepped inside this place, the reflection would become premonition. There would be no Donna in her future then. There would be no future at all.

Streetlight glinted in the reflection's eyes. As Monique retreated backward down the steps to the sidewalk, the reflection seemed to sink into the earth. The image stuck with her as she stepped toward a broad alley, where the music hall faced an office building's gray plaster.

The alley scared her less. There was nothing special here, just one more Manhattan route of grimy asphalt. And Empire Music Hall was nothing special either, even if Gray Hill made her lair underneath. People worked here, cleaned up the place, and took the garbage out. There had to be a service door. It likely hid between buildings.

But as she walked alongside the music hall, the outer wall seemed to grasp for her, its acoustics resonant with lost souls. People had died here—she hadn't heard that anywhere, but it was her gut feeling. Maybe by Gray Hill's enormous hands or by others. Even if there had been no corpse illusion in the entrance's glass doors, this place seemed the type where Monique would fall asleep and wake up to find a maniac tearing out her kidney.

Never again.

A frail light flashed in the alley, and a throat cleared behind it. "Trying to break in, aren't you?"

Beside a dull green dumpster stood a woman wearing a dark jacket and black pants. One hand clutched a smoldering cigarette that reflected in her maroon nail polish; the other stroked her short gray-white hair. She didn't look like security.

"It looks dead, doesn't it?" she asked. "Don't be fooled by the surface. Under its skin, Empire Music Hall is alive." Her free hand left her hair and stuck out toward Monique. "Corene."

Monique became a statue. One foot wanted to turn and run, the other pointed at the music hall's side. If she didn't move, she wouldn't commit to any determined course of action and could pretend all futures remained possible. She'd already taken a big step tonight by following that monster. Trusting a stranger would be like walking into orbit.

Corene lowered her hand and returned to her cigarette. "No need to be cagey, kid. We're both in over our heads. You just don't know it yet."

"I know it. I've seen—" Monique clapped her jaw shut. She'd sound out of her mind.

Corene took a drag, the smoke full of hard choices. "A tall lady, isn't she?"

She'd seen Gray Hill then, meaning she knew secrets, and yet she seemed to be weathering them with a stern approach.

There was no reason to trust her, but if Monique gave nothing, she'd get nothing. She swallowed, throat pressing hard against her scarves, and nodded.

"Then we're both awake to the wonderful world of weird shit." Corene blew smoke. "Lovely. And why are you here?"

Monique stepped closer. "I've always wondered that. Why am I here?"

"Ever get an answer?"

"Doesn't matter. I won't quit being here."

Corene recoiled, but her eyes were alight. "The world

must've thrown you down. Same story around every corner. Did you come here for guidance? That's what they're selling."

"I don't even know what this place is. I'm looking for my—" Monique paused. She wasn't sure how open she should be. "My friend, Donna Ashton. She's disappeared."

"This is a good place for people to disappear." Corene looked wistful. "I've lost someone, same as you. Professor Abraham Clarke, from Queens College."

"Are you a professor too?"

"Do I seem the type?" Corene ran a finger along her sharp cheekbone. Her red nails looked manicured.

Monique dug her nails into her palms. They'd grown over-long, their ends chipped, but she didn't often think about them except when scratching at her arms. Now she felt embarrassed, as if it was her fault that she didn't have a home and job and money and food and Donna.

"I don't know what a professor looks like," Monique said. "But I think you know more than me. How about a way in? I can't really walk through the front door."

"Abraham did." Corene smirked. "He strode up in broad daylight and asked their business. Everyone has their short-comings, even professors. His is that he likes people too much."

"Do you love him?" Monique immediately regretted asking. It was a dumb question, imposing her own circumstances onto someone else.

Corene glanced down the alley. If there were doors, they stood closer to the far end where the alley opened onto another street. "I'm not some doe-eyed grad student chasing a surrogate father figure. Abraham's my friend. My brilliant, clueless friend, and no one else can find him. No one understands him like I do or knows where to look."

Monique stepped closer, into the haze of cigarette smoke. "You're not looking too hard."

"I'm about to quit smoking and I'd like to savor this last one." Corene took one final drag, dropped the cigarette filter beside a shredded candy wrapper, and stamped out the tiny flame. "There, I've quit. Congratulate me."

"I'm proud of you."

Corene stared hard at the dwindling snake of smoke beneath her sneaker. "You're used to rolling with the punches, aren't you? That'll help." She started down the alley. "That tall lady is sloppy when she comes up from underground. I've seen where she pops out." She crouched down behind the dumpster. "And where she goes back down."

A lengthy grate stretched from beside the dumpster. Its rough edges didn't look like it was meant to be opened and shut often, and it hadn't been jammed tight where it belonged. Gray Hill was strong and had probably broken it back when she started her nightly abductions. Why would anyone notice a busted grate? Lots of broken things called the city their home.

Corene stuck her fingers between iron crosshatching and tugged. Monique squatted beside her and yanked back as hard as she could. Her muscles groaned. So did the grate as it slid across pavement. She and Corene moved it just far enough to clear the way, and then they set it on the ground and peered inside.

Darkness pooled in the rectangular hole. Corene lit another cigarette and dropped it inside. It landed maybe six feet down before sputtering out.

"I'll check first," Corene said. She sat at the hole's edge with her legs dangling over, took a deep breath, and then slid herself gently down. Her sneakers clacked against hard linoleum. She grunted, but she didn't sound hurt.

Monique approached the edge. A cavern of bones might lie beneath Empire Music Hall where Gray Hill carried her victims. The monster herself might be waiting. Monique had come this far, but traversing Freedom Tunnel was one thing. She knew the empty place, what it did to her thoughts and nerves. This was uncharted territory. She'd had a lucky break finding the street again after chasing Gray Hill through the underground. Now she couldn't help feeling that if she threw that break away and journeyed back underground, she would never see the surface again. That corpse premonition atop Empire Music Hall's steps would lead her into a bottomless grave, her soul forever falling.

A golden lighter flickered alive in the pool of darkness and cast a glow over Corene's face. Fiery reflections stirred in her hazel eyes. "Scared?" she asked.

Monique glared. Wasn't it obvious?

"You know, kid, fear is just a symptom of old perspective

being broken down. It's the only way we see things in new ways."

Whatever the hell that meant.

Corene stepped back to give room, letting the darkness thicken once more. Monique sat on the opening's edge and let her legs dangle. She tried taking a deep breath and coughed it out.

Hesitation was getting her nowhere. She closed her eyes, slid from the edge, and let the ground swallow her whole.

3
EMPIRE

NARROW WALLS CLOSED IN FROM either side. Gray Hill probably spent this last stretch of each night's excursion in an uncomfortable crawl. No debris blocked the hallway; she had cleared any obstacles weeks ago. Monique didn't worry about tripping over a stray chair. Fortunate, since Corene's lighter made a poor flashlight. It kept sputtering out as they walked, and each time, her thumb had to grind its hissing trigger over and over before the flame returned.

"Some cellar," she whispered, and pointed at open doorways that haunted the underground. "Furnace room. Piping here. Boxes, so probably storage." She raised her head above her lighter and called out: "Abraham?"

Monique glanced back to the hole that was shrinking down the hall behind them. If Gray Hill heard them coming, they wouldn't be able to scrabble up as fast as they'd dropped in.

"I doubt he's nearby," Corene said, lowering her lighter. "That would be too easy, and he'd answer if he heard. That man never shuts up." She took cautious steps forward. "Listen, if there's enough space down here to house the number of people I'm thinking, it could be big. We might get split up."

Monique almost asked who they were, but she was more afraid of Gray Hill.

"If we lose each other, look for a man in his sixties, balding except for scraggly hair running down the sides of his head into his big tough beard. Ever seen a picture of Charles Darwin? That's practically Abraham. He's got a biker's burly build but wears sweaters and jackets with elbow patches. Get the picture?"

"And what if everyone here looks like that?" Monique asked.

"Don't get cute. There'll be elders, but they'll surround themselves with desperate types who need something to believe in. Young, like you. Abraham's not like that." Corene leaned her lighter over one shoulder as if pointing an accusing finger. "Your turn to share. Who should I be watching for?"

"Donna?" Monique couldn't describe her like she wanted: a fiery sun stuffed into a somehow mortal woman. "She's forty, white, blue eyes, brunette except where it's going gray. She has a face like she's annoyed all the time, but in a charming way, like—"

"Going gray?" Corene cut in. "And how old are you?"

Monique shrugged. Did it matter? "Twenty."

"And you're in a relationship with her? Make all the faces you want; when you get to my age, you know your own." Corene smirked. "She sounds a little old for you."

Monique stammered. She hadn't mentioned their relationship. Seldom did anyone guess anything about her, especially after having been around her for all of five minutes. She set her jaw. "That's not really your business," she said.

Corene's lighter flame quivered. "And who would I say is looking for her if you and I are separated?"

"She'll know." If anyone but Monique came looking for Donna, they needed to have their apologies in order. Donna's family had cast her off when Monique was still a child, years before Monique's parents did the same.

"Have it your way. I'll tell Donna I've come on behalf of the uptight young lady in a red cap."

An orange-yellow glow broke the darkness ahead where Corene's lighter reflected off a red metal door. She pressed it open and flicked a wall switch, snapping a dangling overhead bulb to life. It cast pale light down a half-dozen descending stone steps. Another door waited at the bottom.

Deeper and deeper it went.

Corene doused her lighter and started down. "Why did Donna come here?"

Monique still couldn't be sure Donna was even here. This whole excursion might've been risking her life for nothing, but she didn't want to say that. "I think she was taken. Gray Hill's been snatching people off the street for months."

"The tall lady? I didn't find out about her until after Abraham disappeared. He knew the kind of people these were, the history they're playing with, and he couldn't resist knowledge. Their mouthier members might talk, but they're not supposed to tell all. We had star charts and graphs, while they have the raw data of quantum physics, secrets to how the universe plays with time." Corene reached the bottom of the steps and shook her head. "The Worm is too much to explain. Oh, the things people will worship."

Monique paused two steps from the bottom. "The Worm?"

"Ever hear of those UFO cults that wait for aliens to take them to heaven? This is worse. At least for those whackos, none of it's real. These zealots have their monster as proof, and much, much more." Corene reached for the next knob—unlocked. Whoever she feared beneath Empire Music Hall didn't expect company. They might've thought any intruders would be more interested in the expensive instruments and equipment aboveground.

They hadn't anticipated their captives to have loved ones who'd come searching. Did they worship Gray Hill? Monique didn't suppose she could blame them. That monster was unreal, larger than life, a thing Monique wouldn't have believed had she not seen with her own eyes. A soul desperate for higher calling might latch onto such a creature.

The door opened on a stark, cream-colored hallway. Dim fluorescent lights hung overhead, one winking in and out. A couple of doors stood shut along the hall, but nothing else interrupted the walls. Their creamy paint swirled in messy patterns. To stare into them long enough might have conjured shapes and visions, but there wasn't time for that.

Corene marched toward the hall's end, where the path

veered left. "When I say it's too much to explain, I'm not try- ing to insult you," she whispered. "I'm accidentally good at insulting, with everyone. I don't even know you. You might be a physics student who's fallen on hard times. Shit happens."

"I'm not an anything student," Monique said.

"I'm sure you'd stump me on any of your areas of exper- tise."

"It's shortcomings all the way down, promise."

Corene tried one of the knobs in passing, but these doors were locked. "Not even any expertise about Donna? She must be special."

Monique pushed past Corene and toward the hall's end. The pale walls and unhappy lighting reminded her of the building where Marigold & Cohen leased their offices. Had they not met in that damn lobby while Monique was deliver- ing pizza to a smaller office, Donna's life might have stayed on the right track. She'd been a lawyer there for thirteen years. Throwing her aside wasn't fair.

"Donna makes the worst days okay, and the okay days heavenly," Monique said at last.

Corene stepped alongside Monique and regarded her. "You won't quit on her, will you?"

Monique cringed at the thought. "I'm not the kind of girl who quits."

"I've gathered." Corene eyeballed the corner. "Any of these doors might be loaded with people unhappy to see us. Or, we might find Abraham, or Donna." She rubbed two fingers over her lips. "I didn't think this through. I'm no better than he is. He would've talked to the police, but I thought, 'What if it's a misunderstanding?' I couldn't have that, could I?"

Monique's parents, wrongheaded as they could be on so many topics, used to tell her not to trust cops. Living on and off the street since last November had proved them right. No one who lived in Freedom Tunnel had called 9-1-1 about Gray Hill, and no one seemed to care about the missing women. Pulling a college professor's salary, Corene couldn't understand. Money and shelter changed everything.

Maybe Monique had areas of expertise after all. She turned left.

The hall opened into a wide white room. Bright ceiling lights shined around a square vent cover. The floor formed a walkway where another hall opened ahead, and a white staircase descended twenty feet down to a lower level. Green plastic ferns braced the bottom step, and hallways opened to the left and right. Perhaps they would lead to even more descending stairs.

Deeper and deeper, as if there was no bottom.

"They don't hold concerts below street level," Corene said. "The city must know about the lower floors since subway construction would've had to slide around. Call a design simultaneously historic and post-modern, and you can use it to cover up any crime. The public never sees the Worm's secrets and all his followers' religious rites."

That Worm again. Then the people beneath Empire Music Hall didn't worship Gray Hill after all. "But who'd worship worms?" Monique asked, perplexed.

"People will worship anything if they need it," Corene said. "Dangle the Worm on a hook and hungry fish will bite."

Monique's gut roared. The stairway room was all hard surfaces and carried the noise. Right now she would kill for a box of blueberry-flavored Pop-Tarts. They were junk food, but her treasured junk food. Begging the well-dressed man in the subway might've been a ruse, but she could've used a little spare change for food anyway. Now her stomach wanted to claw at her organs and spine. Left as it was, it would eventually digest her vertebrae and then every bone to follow.

Corene glanced at Monique's abdomen, her face, and then gritted her teeth. "You said—what'd you call her, Gray Hill? That she's been snatching people off the street. You've seen it?" She studied Monique again and then reached into her pocket and pulled out a Mars bar. "I was saving this—Abraham's favorite, and mine too—but I think you need it more."

Monique wasn't too proud to take it. She thought she muttered out gratitude before stuffing the chocolatey end in her mouth, but after swallowing the first bite, she couldn't be sure.

"It's been rough, huh? For you and Donna?" Corene gazed out at the white staircase. "You'll have to tell me about it after we find—" She gasped hard and thrashed one arm to the side, grasping the stairway banister. Her voice shrank to a shrill whisper. "Do you see that?"

Monique swallowed the last of the Mars bar and followed Corene's eyes to the ceiling vent. She didn't see anything, but she heard it—a rough scrape, like Gray Hill's cloak.

"Something was watching," Corene said. Her stern veneer melted against her bones. She clasped her trembling hands together. "I thought it was Gray Hill."

"She couldn't fit," Monique said.

"She might not be the only one. There might be ones our size, too." Corene didn't take her eyes off the vent.

Nothing appeared. They wouldn't get anywhere standing here, and if something knew they were in the staircase room, better to go someplace else.

They could still head back. Climbing to the street might be hard, but they still had the physical agency to leave, something that might be taken from them if they were found by Gray Hill or the people who revered worms.

But if they ran, and Donna was here now, then she would never leave. No one else would save her.

Monique hit the first step and then glanced up at Corene. "You can hold my hand."

Corene looked at her intertwined fingers and then scowled. "I'm fifty-one years old. I don't need my hand held." She began down the steps and passed Monique. "You think this is the most dangerous place I've ever been?"

Monique didn't know, but no one trembled like that unless deep down she was terrified.

Corene cleared her throat. "Thank you for not throwing what I said about fear back in my face."

Monique couldn't remember the exact words anyway. She followed down the stairs and tried to keep her eyes off the vent. If something watched from behind its metal slats, there was nothing she could do about it. White linoleum drew closer. When she moved her head, motion blur made stairs, floor, and walls bleed into one.

A red fragment broke the pale haze out the corner of her eye, and she thought of the woman in a red coat, Gray Hill's latest victim. Monique swerved her head again to look.

Someone new stared up at them, her long red hair glaring against the walls. "Excuse me?" Her soft voice bounced off every hard surface.

Corene glared over her shoulder, freezing Monique in place. "You trust me, kid?" she whispered. "Follow my lead and don't believe their smiles. No matter how friendly, loving, and generous they act, if these maniacs catch wise that you don't belong here, they'll tear you limb from limb."

4
ORIENTATION

RED HAIR FLOWED DOWN A white blouse to the waistline of bleached jeans. The young woman looked around Monique's age, almost as thin, and too frail to hurt a fly.

Corene stretched the biggest smile across her face and finished descending the steps. "Hi there, sweetie! We're new and a little lost. Can you help us?"

Monique almost gawked, but the woman was watching. She managed a slender smile.

The woman's eyes narrowed. "Really? I've seen everyone who's been brought in at night."

"We were recruited this afternoon." Corene lowered her head. "For love of the Worm."

An infectious grin burst across the stranger's pale face. She stamped to the bottom of the steps and grabbed Corene's arms. "Newcomers, I love that! We hardly get anyone joining on their own. That must mean the Worm's will is spreading."

"Without a doubt."

The woman let go of Corene and clapped her hands in front of her nose. "I could explode right now, I'm so happy!

Well, no sense leaving you lost. I'll show you around. Would you like to know my name? It was Susan, but I didn't like that, so now I'm Lady, and I can change it because all that ID and records stuff will be washed away by the Worm's infinite oceans. We flow with him and his waters set us free. Neat, huh?" She waved an overzealous arm and stamped back the way she'd come. Her thin brown boots clacked hard against linoleum.

Corene glanced back at Monique, briefly dropped her smile into a scowl, and then picked it up and followed Lady.

Monique wasn't sure she could smile that wide. She trailed behind Corene.

Lady's enthusiastic footsteps faded into a softer hallway. The carpet's orange-brown fibers felt dull beneath the white walls, where patterns swirled in the paint. Black doors lined the hallway, paused where it forked left, and then continued on toward its far end.

"We sleep here," Lady said. "It's almost ceremony time, so we'll have to find your beds later. There's a bathroom on each end." She clapped again. "Oh, but there's so much to see. The elevator to the Sunless Palace, the dining hall, the ceremony chamber, the practice room—well, that's halfway behind the dorms." She pointed to the fork in the hall.

"What do we practice?" Monique asked.

Lady's eyebrow climbed her forehead. "The only thing that matters. The song that pierces the universe."

"Oh, right." Monique felt Corene's muscles tensing.

But Lady didn't seem to care. Her eyes turned to the ceiling. "They built the under-levels before they built the music hall, way before I was born. I like to think of the surface music as inspiration. They play above, we sing below."

A toad of anxiety planted itself in Monique's throat, and her scarves now seemed too tight. She hadn't been up for singing since she began sleeping beside the empty place. Even before that, Donna used to coax a song out of her only through begging or getting Monique tipsy. She wasn't sure she'd sound good enough anymore for Corene's charade.

"I have an idea!" Lady spun around to face them. "Do you know about the twin histories?"

"Yes," Corene said while Monique shook her head.

Monique fought the toad out of her throat. "I mean, I

wasn't paying good attention when they told us. I'm sorry."

Lady glanced between them. "That's okay. Actually, it's great. I love telling it." She turned from them and headed for the fork in the hallway.

Corene glared at Monique. "Limb from limb," she whispered. They followed Lady.

Swirling paint patterns decorated the next hallway branch. Its only door stood shut at the end, where a vibrant hum climbed and fell from the other side. Shadows seemed to quiver in the paint with each changing note. Monique rubbed her eyes and tugged her beanie down a little tighter.

"Everything started with the seer who loved the stars," Lady said, stroking her fingers across one wall's indistinct patterns. They might have been dots for stars and dashes for figures. They might have been nothing at all. "He wasn't human like us. His kind were more like birds who sang in the morning to let each other know they'd survived the night. But he was different. He sang at dusk to tell the stars he'd missed them. And one night, the stars sang back. That was when the Worm found the world."

Each step brought Lady closer to the door. Monique felt compelled to follow, the notes being sung behind the door stirring her blood. The hum didn't sound like a real song. She couldn't say what made certain sounds into a real song, but these weren't doing it.

Lady glanced over her shoulder. "Do you know about Pangaea?" she asked.

Corene piped up. "The ancient supercontinent. All continents were at one point a single landmass until shifting tectonic plates began to spread them apart 175 million years ago." She didn't look unnerved by the song. Maybe she didn't like music and couldn't tell the difference between classical, pop, and universe-piercing arias.

"For us, yes, Pangaea is long gone." Lady stroked another white mural. It might have been a world surrounded by stars, or any circle surrounded by dots, or chaotic nothingness. "For the seer's kind, Pangaea never broke apart. It was still around all those millions of years to when the Worm found them. He carved out the Great Pangaea Kingdoms to be ruled by his kings, and the seer became the highest king of all. That was the First Coming of the Worm.

"But decades later, at the Second Coming, the kings betrayed the Worm. All he asked for was one of their daughters, a little bride to call his own, and they wouldn't give him one, not even the seer. So, he threw down their crowns and broke the seer; we call him King of the Broken Throne now. And that wasn't all. The Worm reached back millions of years and smashed the continents so their kind would never be.

"Time changed then. The seer's people became a shadow of a memory of Earth. They never happened." Lady spun around and clapped her hands together. "And then we happened instead. Aren't we the luckiest?"

Creamy paint rippled with song. One circle stretched into two prongs of overlapping circles. Depictions of a parallel history hid in the wall paint, the world stagnant in one set of years and changing in another, the stuff of comic books and sci-fi movies. Monique had heard of people who believed in space aliens, but never like this. Something about painting it into the walls where they slept gave the idea fingers to reach for her, as much nothing and yet all-consuming as the empty place in Freedom Tunnel. The paint depicted infinity. It was also formless slop, each shape as meaningless as the bare space between them.

Everything or nothing, Monique couldn't tell. The paint would not keep still.

"Now we wait for the Third Coming of the Worm," Lady said. Had she been talking while Monique stared at the wall? Another mystery. "And when we sing true, it'll happen. Sorry, you probably knew some parts of that, but I get carried away. Which is good, right? The Worm is infinite, so our love has to be infinite to keep up. It's like I always say, you can't love the Worm too much, right?"

Monique's breath came out shakily. "Never."

"Then it really is a religion?" Corene asked. Her fingers twitched together as if she wanted to take notes.

"Everyone sees the world their own way," Lady said. "The Worm changes you, and the biggest change is coming. The meek shall inherit, right? I think someone said that once."

A phone rang behind the door, and the humming ceased. The silence settled under Monique's skin, almost peaceful. She eyed the paint for movement and patterns—all became still. There was nothing to see.

The doorknob clicked. A bald, muscular man about Donna's age emerged, wearing a white suit. A teenage boy in denim followed him.

Lady clapped again. She seemed to like that sound as much as any song. "Mr. Bouchard! Israel! How's practice?"

"His song is a pure needle unspoiled by human doubt," Bouchard said, whose voice was a gong that pounded in Monique's ears. "He has his confidence back, ready to pierce the universe. We're headed for the ceremony hall."

"Already?" Lady asked. "I'd prayed for—oh well, you know better than I do. We can't keep the others waiting." She herded everyone back to the dormitory hall, where Bouchard took the lead.

Nothing trembled in the wall paint at their passing, and Monique was starting to feel silly. The halls took them around another corner and past a row of shut doors.

Lady walked beside Israel, excitedly asking about his singing technique. When he didn't perk up, she nudged him with her elbow. "What's wrong? You're rejoining the choir today. You'll flow with the Worm in front of Mr. Bouchard and the other preachers."

Corene cut in. "Don't you mean kings?"

"That would defy the Worm's will," Lady said, looking back. "Kings are kings; the rest of us serve in our own way."

"Some serve more than others," Corene muttered.

She wasn't making sense. The song that had eaten at Monique's nerves had been nothing but choir practice. She'd let paranoia mix with Corene's wrongheaded warnings. These people talked weird, sure, but they seemed harmless, maybe unaware that a monster lived beneath Empire Music Hall and grabbed people off the street. This seemed an encouraging environment, unfamiliar and yet welcoming.

"Try a happier face, please," Corene said. "What's the matter?"

"They're not hurting anyone," Monique said.

"Didn't you listen? Don't trust their smiles. They might look harmless on the surface, but healing and harm can be a matter of perspective."

"But it's just pretend."

"Also a matter of perspective."

Monique scowled, ruffling her beanie. "Don't tell me you

believe this stuff."

"Not the way they do," Corene said. "Don't look at me that way, kid. I'll explain later."

Monique stepped a little quicker to keep up with Lady and the others. Linoleum replaced the carpet as they stepped into a wider room. High doorways opened to the left and right. Chaos swirled in the paint on the far side of the room, where a crowd of maybe a hundred or so bustled and chatted. They wore ordinary clothes, same as most anyone who walked New York City's streets, almost like they were ordinary people. Their faces looked cheerful, and their pleasant chatter bounded off the open hall's hard surfaces.

Beneath the noise, Israel was saying something that Monique couldn't make out.

Lady was closer though, and a little louder. "Don't be ashamed. Palace duty is an honor."

Israel shrugged. "I know. It just doesn't feel right that we're all together up here, but she has to stay down there alone."

She. That could've meant anyone, but Donna lit Monique's world. What did Israel mean by *down there*? They were already at least one story beneath street level. There had to be deeper places hidden beneath Empire Music Hall. Lady had mentioned an elevator.

She nudged Israel's arm again. "No one below can come up here. They haven't been dismissed. And we can't stay down there like them; it's too dangerous. Listen, the Worm's will is the best thing that's ever existed. We have to follow it."

Monique's mouth opened, closed. She didn't know how to ask about this without making the others suspicious.

Corene rescued her. "What's below?" she asked. "What does that mean?"

Lady smirked. "Down the grand elevator to the Sunless Palace. You know, Old Time."

"No, I don't know. Who's down there?"

"Well, the Gray Maiden, that old man, and of course—"

Corene grabbed Lady's arm. "What old man? Abraham Clarke?"

Lady's smirk shrank. "Do you know him?"

Do. A good word, putting Abraham in the present tense. Maybe Donna was alive, too, in the Sunless Palace of Old

Time, standing next to Neverland, the Ark of the Covenant, and any other important-sounding titles this Worm cult could dredge up.

The hall's chatter died, but Corene didn't seem to notice. "I want to see Abraham."

Lady tugged at her arm. "You're hurting me." She looked to the faces surrounding them and then fixed on Bouchard. "Can anyone help her? She's new and wants to know about the visitor."

"New since when?" Bouchard asked. "We aren't welcoming anyone who doesn't sing unless the Gray Maiden brings them by mistake. So you must've auditioned."

"Sing for us," Lady said, clasping her hands together. She seemed to be looking past Monique and Corene, her eyes unfocused and reverent. "Do it."

Corene dropped her hand from Lady's arm. Maybe she was realizing how careless she'd been to make a scene. Her gravelly voice hummed, not to sing, but uncertain what to say.

Monique opened her mouth and sang a rising, wordless warm-up note. If she'd stopped to think, nothing would have come out, but now the tune spilled unbidden and desperate. Singing well herself should've been enough to vouch for Corene. It was only fair.

Indistinct faces nodded. Bouchard looked over Corene's head.

Monique didn't want to look back, but she couldn't help herself. In one motion, she pivoted on her feet and slid her fingers up her jacket sleeve, where they grabbed her switchblade.

"OOH!"

The aural blast quaked through Monique's bones. Her switchblade tumbled down her shuddering arm, out her sleeve, and onto the floor.

Gray Hill towered over her. Ceiling lights shrank her shadow to just beneath and behind her. Taking two steps closer to the crowd would've given her away. Her silvery talons twinkled against the ungodly pale walls. Thick cloth still shrouded her face, but a shadow inside hinted at a toothy snout and bristly skin that might've been coated in hair, feathers, or something nightmarish.

One sickle claw tapped linoleum beside the fallen

switchblade. Her birdlike legs eased backward, letting her crouch for a closer look. She might've had a bird's fascination for shiny objects.

Lady grabbed Monique's arm and tugged her into the thick of the crowd. "You don't want to see this. Let the Gray Maiden do her thing."

Faces closed in around them. Monique thought she should try to fight, but her legs wanted to run from the tall lady, Gray Hill, Gray Maiden, whatever this monster was called. Without meaning to, she let the crowd pull her away.

Still, she twisted her neck to look over her shoulder.

Corene trembled from head to toe. She turned to follow the crowd, but her legs wobbled, and the Gray Maiden's hands were quick. Long fingers latched around Corene's middle and yanked her off the floor. The switchblade lay useless in her shadow. Seeing the Gray Maiden's enormous height and limbs in clear light, Monique knew for certain a cut would've only pissed her off.

"Stop her," Monique muttered to Lady.

"I don't tell her what to do," Lady said with a laugh in her voice. "The Gray Maiden is her own person. Only kings command her."

Corene hacked out a rough cough. "I didn't come here to sing or die," she snapped. "I'll find Abraham and then—bastards!" She wheezed hard, gasped again, and then she was quiet, same as the woman from Freedom Tunnel. Maybe the Gray Maiden's awful hands had that effect on the human body, squeezing out all air until her victim became a limp doll, easy to carry.

Monique almost shouted, but there was no point. She'd only give herself away and then be taken too. "Where are they going?" she asked. Too many people crowded around her now. She couldn't see Corene anymore, only the Gray Maiden hunching behind the procession.

"To Gray's home below in Old Time," Lady said. "You'll see it someday; we all will. She has her chutes and we have the grand elevator, but all roads in life lead to the Worm in the end."

If that was true, everything would be fine. Far as Lady, Bouchard, and their group knew, Monique was one of them. All roads led to the Worm? Then she'd find the grand elevator, Old Time, and bring Corene back.

And with any luck, she'd find Donna below and bring her back, too.

5
NIGHTLY CEREMONY

THE PROCESSION FILED THROUGH A tall doorway
and split to either side of the room, where they sat in wooden
chairs to the left or climbed onto the broad platform to the
right. Lady led Monique onto the platform and toward the far
wall opposite the doorway, where sickly white surfaces halted
at a sheet of beautiful midnight blue. No chaos swirled in its
paint. It stood flat and unblemished, the only pure and peaceful wall beneath Empire Music Hall.

Monique couldn't take her eyes off it. She only realized
Lady was talking when her outstretched arm grazed the edge
of sight. She was pointing people out and naming them. Mr.
Something, Ms. Whoever, and someone else and some other,
a blur of names and faces that Monique couldn't piece together. There had to be over a hundred people in the room,
too many to memorize. Lady talked a lot, but she said little.

Israel and a few dozen others filled the platform, gathering
a motley of faces from every corner of the city, with Monique
standing closest to the blue wall. She wondered if any of their
families knew they were here. Or if they cared.

When everyone on the other side of the room had seated themselves, Bouchard stood up in front of them. "The choir is gathered, and the ceremony will commence," he said. "We'll call the low end of the song tonight." He waved at the doorway.

Monique leaned her face toward Lady's hair and whispered, "Are we the choir?"

Lady tittered. It was enough of an answer.

"What about Bouchard?" Monique asked. "Is he in charge?"

"You're so silly," Lady said, smirking. "Mr. Bouchard conducts the ceremony, but only the Worm and his kings are in charge. You should pay more attention—uh." Her smirk faded and her forehead creased. "Huh. I don't know your name."

Bouchard clapped his hands, commanding silence. Lady might not have thought he was kingly, but authority breathed off men like him, almost a smell that Monique couldn't name. It reminded her of when she'd visit the lobby of Marigold & Cohen for secret meetings with Donna. Those lawyers didn't rule the world, but the power of their money and positions crackled between them and their followers.

Here, that power might have been the will of the Worm.

Four stragglers traipsed through the doorway, dragging with them a woman who wore a familiar red coat. They led her down the open floor between the chairs and platform, toward the empty blue wall, and rested her at the room's center. She had dangled unconscious from the Gray Maiden's hands earlier this evening, but now her eyes were open, and she sat on her knees. She seemed strangely calm, but by her heaving chest, Monique could tell she was exhausted.

Bouchard cleared his throat. "Each of you came to us with a purpose," he said, his voice booming. "You felt something unripe about our world, its composition started by the universe and yet incomplete, and you didn't find the composer in God, Buddha, or Benjamin Franklin."

A polite chuckle traveled Bouchard's side of the room. Lighting the floors beneath Empire Music Hall couldn't be free, and housing people in this city was never cheap. Some of them had to have money, or they knew others who did. They sat here giggling while their pet monster snatched women off the street.

It boiled Monique's blood. They didn't have enough power above; they had to come down here and weave nonsense to justify themselves. They might not have called themselves the Worm's kings, but blaming their god's will and claiming divine right was self-styled royalty just the same. Corene was wrong; they weren't dangerous because they could tear someone limb from limb. They were dangerous because they were too high on their own fantasies to think straight, and no one would question them.

Bouchard waited for the chuckling to die and then carried on. "Most of all, you know that whatsoever your walk of life, high or low, you deserve more. And now you've come to get it. The Third Coming of the Worm fast approaches. When we offer up the new Bride of the Worm and our talented choir sings the song that pierces the universe, everyone here will become a king of Earth, strong as the first." He clapped his hands again, shaking Monique's nerves. "Hail the founder of the ceremony, the seer who was crowned, the King of the Broken Throne. Without him, the Worm would not have found this world. Without the Broken King's betrayal, the Worm would not have split Pangaea. Without the sundering of Pangaea, the human race would not exist. Hail the Broken King! Hail the almighty Worm!"

"Hail the almighty Worm!" The chant rang over the chairs and slammed across the platform.

Monique bit the insides of her cheeks not to snicker. If it weren't for the Gray Maiden's monstrous nature giving some meat to their words, they would be nothing but another mound of crackpots. Who had ever heard of worship for a worm? None of these people could've survived the streets.

Bouchard turned to the room's center. "Phoebe Clarence here isn't who we're looking for. She hasn't the choir's skill, and she refuses to flow with the Worm's will by choice. It is time we return her to the universe, exposed to ever-present infinity."

Phoebe didn't look at him. She hugged her coat tighter around her. "Please, please."

Bouchard raised his hands and flashed a smile at the choir, that same *this won't hurt a bit* smile that Doctor Sam had given before Monique's operation. Ice threatened her blood, but the choir stood straight beside her, and she almost felt the empty blue wall stand at attention with them. She managed to follow suit while her eyes kept wandering to Phoebe.

"Minor notes, monophonic," Bouchard said. "We won't sing the whole song. Newcomers, follow along."

Monique hadn't been caught singing in front of people since last summer. She'd had a home then, and Donna, and they'd stayed out late at Coney Island where they met a girl named Rhiannon. Donna was in a goofy mood that night and seemed to think that name was the coolest thing in the world. They spent the next three hours running around, drinking, and singing Fleetwood Mac, Renaissance, any music Donna had been into when she was in her mid-twenties and finishing up law school. By morning, she and Monique were sitting on the boardwalk crooning Rhiannon's name over and over, the rest of the lyrics forgotten. Rhiannon herself had left them long before that.

When Bouchard swung his hands down, the choir opened their mouths as one and began a droning, insect-like hum. It rang inside Monique's head, her skull turning glassy and vibrating to the note's frequency. The song stirred inside her. Holding it in was harder than letting it out.

Her jaw snapped open wetly, and she belted out a high-pitched aria. She forced it a few octaves lower to match the choir. Their hum synchronized, and then began to sway and flow, notes climbing and falling like the tide. Monique's voice drifted on those waves.

Phoebe doubled over and hugged her middle. She reminded Monique of the nights she'd cry outside Freedom Tunnel, unwilling to move in case the empty place might steal her sobs. "Please, don't." Phoebe sounded in pain.

"Harmonize with the universe," Bouchard said. His arms swung in motions that probably meant something to the practiced members of the choir, but nothing to Monique. She tried to follow their hum. "Fold the notes into purity."

Phoebe's eyes squeezed shut as all sound died in her mouth. She had to be making noise, her lips still moved, but the choir's song drowned her anguish. Her shadow stretched behind her, crossed the floor toward the empty wall, and climbed across midnight blue paint until it stood as tall as the Gray Maiden.

Monique guessed someone was manipulating the ceiling

lights. Shadows didn't move on their own.

"Stronger!" Bouchard bellowed. Veins mapped city blocks across his bald head. "This is only one side of the song. If you can't master this, how will you master its completion? Impress me, singers. Impress the Worm."

The choir obeyed. Their hum rang in Monique's ears; she had to sing louder to fight it.

Phoebe's spine arched backward. Ceiling light poured over her face and slipped down her open throat. She looked to the empty wall now, upside-down, head lolling over her shoulders. One arm hugged tight against her chest. The other reached for the entrance, the choir, anything, anyone who might help. An earthquake tore through her, every limb shaking.

The song was doing it, Monique realized. The harsher its hum, the harder Phoebe quaked. One singer's warping the wall paint earlier had been a forgettable parlor trick compared to the full choir's cruel magic.

The song was causing pain, and Monique was part of it. She tried to shut her mouth and swallow the song, but to resist made her teeth rattle, her skull clinging too tight. One foot slid toward the empty wall. Maybe she couldn't stop singing, but she could try to leave the ceremony room.

Phoebe seemed to move, too. Like her shadow, her body stretched across the floor. Her red coat echoed toward the empty wall in transparent afterimages, the same optical effect of waving a hand in front of someone's eyes too fast, but it was happening to her entire body. Her lips moved where she sat solid at the floor's center, and the change echoed down each Phoebe-shaped fragment, a ripple of patterns across a dozen blurring faces.

Monique couldn't hear a word—the hum was too loud, inside and out—but somehow she could tell that Phoebe was praying.

Monique's foot slid off the platform. She had to get out. No one would stop her from creeping along the empty wall to the far side of the room, sneaking behind the chairs, and out the entrance.

All eyes were on Phoebe, being stretched through time, narrowing. Dying.

Monique took two steps along the wall and rebounded off

the air as if she'd hit a hard surface. Her mind grasped at Lady's comment about whoever was under the music hall. *They haven't been dismissed.* Monique tried again, but the air between Phoebe and the midnight blue wall repelled her. She tried again, and her legs swiveled, almost dropping her to the floor.

Cold seeped across her skin, the deepest she'd ever known. The kind of cold shape that clawed at her dreams. The song quit rattling in her head, as if likewise repelled. "No, that can't be," she whispered under her breath.

The empty place was here. She had crossed blocks of Manhattan from Freedom Tunnel and yet it had wormed through the city's underbelly to chase her.

"What do you want?" she snapped. "What are you?" There was no answer. No one else seemed to notice it, same as in Freedom Tunnel. It was sucking up the choir's song, Phoebe's prayers, Monique's questions, filling itself with their sound. Not even dust would touch the empty place, but it was taking their music.

It was eating Phoebe.

Any remnants of the hum in Monique's throat shattered into a scream. She didn't care about sneaking anymore. She darted past poor Phoebe, whose form was losing focus and fading into thin air, and through the ceremony room's doorway.

The room was not quiet behind Monique. Without the hum ringing in her skull, even clamping her hands over her ears couldn't stop the sound of Phoebe being pulled apart between the empty place and time itself. She was screaming, but the sound synchronized with the choir.

And then it was gone. Monique didn't need to look back to tell that Phoebe was gone, too.

Bouchard bellowed once again. "Even in death, we still serve the Worm. Our souls are tethered to him, for he is the fountain from which we spring. She is with him now. None will be dismissed until the Third Coming of the Worm, a world where we are kings."

The choir's hum broke into cheers.

6
CARVERS

MONIQUE FELT ONE LEG GIVE out beneath her. This past winter when she'd slogged through snowbanks, hardly able to walk, Donna had held her up, but there was no Donna here. The choir might have murdered her already. Monique would have no one to save. She stumbled, falling.

Lady caught her arm. "It's okay," she said. "The Worm asks a lot, I know, but you can't just leave. Someday we'll sing the real thing and pierce the universe. There'll be no running then."

"They killed her," Monique rasped. She wanted Lady to stop touching but couldn't pull away. Every muscle felt limp. "They killed her, we killed her."

"No."

"She's part of its nothing now." Hot tears flooded Monique's cheeks. She tried to swallow the burning lump in her throat. "We fed her to the empty place."

"No, no." Lady smiled wide and shook her head. "Most of the universe is empty. We feel stretches of the Worm, and she's with him now, and he's full and infinitellsetsafreee—"

Her words smashed together and thinned like Phoebe across time, becoming nothing.

Monique's stomach turned. She covered her mouth, tried to swallow again, but hot bile surged. She turned desperate eyes to Lady, who pointed at a door to the right. Monique banged through it into a tan bathroom full of stalls and sinks. She smelled cleaning product and it only made her more nauseous. She rushed into a stall, fell to her knees, and vomited into the toilet bowl.

Lady stomped into the stall from behind. "There, now. You'll be fine." She grasped Monique's hair and began pulling it back. Fingers crossed the beanie's rim.

"Don't touch it!" Monique coughed until her throat was clear. "Just go."

"Oh." Lady slipped out of the stall. She hovered near the sinks for a moment and then left the restroom.

Monique faced the toilet and waited, but nothing else surged up her throat. Corene's candy bar had been her only food in two days, and now it was gone to waste. For all the clawing in her gut, she couldn't stomach seeing Phoebe being torn apart.

Limb from limb, as Corene had warned. What had she already known before she led the way into this hellhole? What had happened to Phoebe could happen to anyone. One wrong night in Freedom Tunnel and the empty place might've chewed Monique the same way. What was wrong with this city?

She reached up and flushed. She wished the toilet could drag Empire Music Hall down its pipes too, one little hole draining all this merry evil. If only it were that simple.

She crawled off the floor and realized she had to pee, too. It might've been out of fear more than any other reason, but the need came sudden and without question. She hadn't been through enough pain tonight, it seemed. Before Doctor Sam, this never used to hurt, but urinating had become a dice roll in agony ever since. Sometimes she rolled high and felt mild discomfort at worst. Other times, she rolled low.

Tonight she rolled burning snake eyes. She bit her lip not to scream, but her teeth could only muffle so much. A shriek rattled up her already stinging throat. She clasped her hands tight over open lips and screamed hard into her palms. The scream didn't finish until she did. She collapsed against the back of the toilet and gasped in and out, forcing her heart to settle.

It was over. She staggered out of the stall and washed her hands.

The good doctor had seemed like a miracle, offering out-of-hospital surgery on the cheap. "I'm Samuel Reinhart," he'd said, "but everyone calls me Doctor Sam." His smile could light the world, Monique had thought. She wondered how many storage unit surgeries he'd botched, first carving up a patient in the area of their body that was agreed upon, quicker and sloppier than they wanted, and then helping himself to a kidney, damn the consequences. If any surgeries ended in blood-spattered disasters, no skin off his back. Pack up, move, rinse the blood off his hands, repeat.

Monique had been a unique disaster. Donna had laid her on that freezing table, surrounded by concrete walls and sto-len medical equipment that beeped and churned. "A couple hours," she said, her hand on Monique's cheek being the only warmth in that dim room. "I'll see you then, Mon Amour."

When Monique finally woke up, two days had passed in feverish nightmare. All she remembered from that time was sweat and pain. Donna later explained about Doctor Sam's side practice of selling kidneys on the black market, how she'd taken his own scalpel and turned it against him to save Monique. She'd had to call an ambulance they couldn't afford, which rushed Monique to an expensive emergency room, where they only treated her botched surgery and infection un-til she was stable. Once she could walk, she had to go.

She had hobbled alongside Donna into a New York winter midnight, icy flakes hitting her skin and melting down her hospital gown. The Salvation Army was a no-go as always for people like them. They ended up in the Fujianese Church of the Transfiguration in Chinatown, stepping in during mid-night mass and lying along the back pews. The kind pastor invited them deeper inside to escape the cold and never asked who they were or what they were running from, but beyond that, he couldn't help them. Donna only found a homeless shelter by luck the next day.

A week passed before Monique could bear to eat solid food. Her insides burned every time she relieved herself. While she could guess the damage by touch, yet another week passed before she dared look at what Doctor Sam had hacked between her thighs or the stitches that ran along her left side and back. He'd been an inch from taking her kidney. The emergency room medical personnel had patched her up soundly, but they weren't plastic surgeons and it wasn't their job to make her pretty.

Donna had stayed through it all, right until the shelter closed down and she disappeared. Monique had moved into Freedom Tunnel after that, discovered the empty place, and spent long days searching for Donna.

And now these people had her. They were carvers, like Doctor Sam, all greedy fingers and knives in their smiles. Monique couldn't let them do to Donna what they'd done to Phoebe, and God knew how many other people, if they hadn't already.

They weren't entirely delusional. The empty place was real; so was Gray Hill. Every old ghost story might be real, too. Monique could believe there was an almighty Worm god who crawled through time, smashed continents, and slithered in starlight. These people were killing for that starlight, and they loved every drop of blood.

At least now Monique knew what she was dealing with. She could be ready for it or try to be. There was no mouthwash here; she gargled sink water to clear the taste of vomit, but nothing could wash the death song out of her throat. She would always taste the piercing of the universe. Best not to show it. She needed to work these people a little more for now. She took a breath and then stepped out of the restroom.

Lady was waiting, her lips pursed in concern, her wrists crossed below the waist of her bleached jeans. "All better?" she asked.

Monique forced her most pleasant smile. "Where's the grand elevator?"

7
THE GRAND ELEVATOR

"WE SHOULD REALLY BE GETTING back," Lady said, but she led them toward the dorms anyway. She kept looking over her shoulder as if expecting someone to come chasing her down. "I told Mr. Bouchard I'd just be a minute to check on you."

"I feel like the Worm wants me to see the elevator," Monique said. "The ceremony was so full of love." She would've vomited again had there been anything left in her stomach. "I'm meant to see it. *We're* meant to go there right now. Don't you feel it?"

Lady's eyes sparkled. "I think I feel it too." Her pace quickened.

She had cheered along with the rest of the choir at Phoebe's death, but no one could enjoy killing this much. She, Israel, and others had to have been brainwashed into complacence and changed by the Worm. Helping them was beyond Monique's power. The song that pierced the universe would impale them on the empty place if their kings saw fit.

She eyed the linoleum for her switchblade, but it was

nowhere to be seen. Someone must have grabbed it when the Gray Maiden took Corene away, maybe even the Gray Maiden herself.

Lady led them back through the carpeted dorm hall, where she'd told the story of the seer and the Worm—Monique didn't look in case the paint began to writhe—and into the white staircase room. Their footsteps echoed off every wall. Monique glanced at the ceiling vent for whatever Corene had seen earlier, but its slats remained dark and empty. She hurried next to Lady in case that was about to change. Their footsteps went quiet in the next carpeted hallway.

"Was she your friend?" Lady asked.

Who did she mean, Corene or Phoebe? Monique shook her head.

"My first ceremony scared me, too." Lady sighed as if recalling from eons ago. "No one's fed to whatever you called it. The empty place. That woman back there—"

"Phoebe," Monique said.

"Right. The Worm is pure, untainted by flesh. The only way we'll join him is to shed the flesh and become pure ourselves. You wouldn't drink a glass of water if it had a drop of blood in it, right?" Lady had clearly never been so thirsty. "It's the same. He needs purity. It only seems empty because the universe is making room to accommodate him. The song wipes our flesh away and welcomes our pure selves to the Worm. We'll all join him someday."

Monique licked her lips and thought of Freedom Tunnel. Just what had she slept beside?

Lady nudged her elbow into Monique's arm. "Don't be so glum. We're all pieces of a greater world in the making. History belongs to us."

Monique didn't think so. The Worm empowered kings, not queens. The authority that crackled off Bouchard and his side of the ceremony room didn't spark the same in the choir. Some of the Worm's servants sat in chariots, while others were horses. No meek would inherit this world.

The carpeted hallway opened into a narrow white passage, where glaring walls made seeing turns and corners difficult. Nothing seemed distinct, and without a guide, it would've been easy to get lost beneath Empire Music Hall. Worse, white paint pretended to hold patterns like before. Monique focused on the safe, boring grout lines between linoleum squares.

"It won't always be like this," Lady said. "Into the Sunless Palace we'll go. The wounds of this world will be unmade, so says the king."

"Scars never go away," Monique said.

"They will when the Worm remakes the world. The Worm changes you."

"How does he do that?"

"Same as he's changing you now." Lady's face looked almost lovesick. "His will is gravity, and we can't help falling for him. He wants, and we think. That's how we know who's meant to be a king, how you know you need to see the elevator."

Monique guessed that was true. Kings were liars, too.

"Nothing really holds still; even the world is always spinning, like clay on a pottery wheel. Earth will be unmade, remade, and we'll be changed into new things." Lady clapped her hands, and their echo became thunderous applause. "The Worm has a special shape for me."

It was hard not to envy her enthusiasm. "You're so lucky," Monique said.

"And you, too." Lady turned and smiled. "The Worm changes everyone. I wonder what you'll become."

Monique felt suddenly transparent and glanced down at herself. Beneath her clothes, she was scarred from Doctor Sam's touch. She tried to quell the quivering curiosity inside her.

She couldn't. "When's the Worm supposed to do all this?"

"At his Third Coming." Lady's next sigh was almost a song. "We'll ready the bride, gather in the Sunless Palace, and sing the song that pierces the universe. The Worm knows when he'll be back, even if we don't."

Down in the Sunless Palace. Donna was below, if she was here at all, every road leading to her and the Worm. A god and his bride. They were going to do to Donna what they had done to Phoebe, but to some grander magnitude. The Worm's ultimate ceremony.

Monique could somewhat relate. She would've married Donna, too, if possible. They would've made wonderful wives together.

49

The narrow hall ended in another high-ceilinged room. Sparse furniture and plastic ferns lined the walls, where messy paint cast the cosmos in white. Another vent watched from above. Monique thought she saw something move inside, but after she blinked, it looked empty.

"Can we hurry?" she asked. If the ceiling hid sliding shadows and watchful eyes, she wanted to get far away from them.

"I hope it's okay to show you the elevator so soon," Lady said, but she picked up her pace. "I'm a little nervous."

That wouldn't do. If Lady was nervous, she might run them back to the choir and its leaders. Best to keep her focused. "What's it like below?" Monique asked.

"Well, there's the elevator tunnel, and the channels that Gray uses." Lady looked to be counting items of interest on her fingers. "The Sunless Palace, the Chamber of Old Time—Mr. Bouchard says the whole underground flows from there. Lots of cultures have found it, but we're the last, and everyone along the way has respected its purity. Pretty neat, huh? It's like the Worm wills us to understand him." That sounded like a useful skill. Lady gave another hand clap. "We're here!"

Twin vertical shafts ran down the wall from ceiling to either side of steel double doors. No decorations marked the metalwork. The elevator didn't look particularly grand, but symbols patterned the wall paint much clearer than anywhere else. Monique made out a crooked line connecting seven points, the constellation of a worm formed between stars.

A service panel and two round buttons stuck out beside the doors. She pressed one, and unseen gears began to thrum.

"We're going down?" Lady asked. "I thought you just needed to see it."

Monique shrugged. "I'm following the Worm's will."

Lady stared for a long moment as the clank of elevator gears counted the seconds. Then she smiled. "I'm so happy for you. Newcomers don't usually catch wind of him so quickly, not even me. Okay then, no permission, we're bold and ready and doing this." She craned her neck toward one vertical shaft and took a deep breath. "Oooh-oooh!"

Monique gaped. "What are you doing?"

Lady's neck settled over her shoulders. "I called the Gray Maiden to meet us at the bottom. Nobody goes into Old Time without her. It's too dangerous in the realm of the old kings."

"What does that mean? Why do we need her?"

"Because there are worse things than kings down there."

Monique reached up her sleeve on instinct, found no switchblade, and raked jagged nails down her arm. There was no telling what that monster would do. She had to know Monique didn't belong here and had chosen Corene between a woman who could sing and another who couldn't. Between Monique and Lady, the Gray Maiden would figure things out.

The room offered no hiding places. The chairs were thin and useless, and the vent was too high up. A shadow swept across its black slats.

"Are there other monsters like the Gray Maiden?" Monique asked.

Lady scoffed. "She's not a monster. She's just a different kind of person, a refugee of Old Time. Lots of New Yorkers are refugees from somewhere or another. Why not another Earth?"

Monique tried again. "Are there other people like her?"

"Not that I know of." Lady pressed her knuckles against her chin. "Do you think it's fair they made Gray learn English, but we won't learn her language? It's like singing, but tougher. I'm trying to get better at it so we can talk, and maybe she won't feel lonely. We don't even know what she calls herself." She turned to Monique, pivoting her chin across her knuckles. "Actually, I don't know what you call yourself, either. What's your name?"

Monique almost said Phoebe, who had given her name—how else could Bouchard know it?—and now she was dead. That seemed a bad omen.

Monique didn't answer, wouldn't even look at Lady, just watched the elevator light up and its double doors slide open. It seemed safer to hide every piece of herself that she could. Empire Music Hall was greedy. Give it an inch and it would take an island. Her name was worth more than an inch anyway. Even Donna rarely called her Monique; more often Mon Amour. She was silly like that.

"Weird smell," Monique said, stepping inside. "Kind of dewy." It wasn't true; the elevator had a copper smell, but she didn't know what to say.

Lady didn't either. She pursed her lips and followed inside. The doors closed in an airy kiss. The elevator trembled around them, cleared its mechanical throat, and then sank into the earth.

Lady stretched her arms high, pressing fingertips against the ceiling, and leaned over Monique. "Why won't you tell me your name?" Her voice came melodic, but there was something coy in it, too.

Monique focused hard on the elevator doors. The engine hummed through every wall, a metal choir of its own. "Why do you want to know so bad?" she asked.

"Because we're friends, and I told you mine." Lady leaned a little deeper. "Or do you think mine's a fake because I chose it?"

"I'd never think that." Monique willed the doors to open; she didn't care which floor.

Lady took a step closer, placing one boot toe between Monique's sneakers. "You're looking at the doors, but there aren't any stops on the way. It's all rock between the surface and Old Time. Express route to the Sunless Palace."

Monique retreated, and her back hit hard steel. The elevator seemed to shrink the deeper it went. She was stuck here, and Lady was a stranger, nothing like a friend at all. Monique couldn't remember her last true friend.

Lady shoved Monique flat against the elevator wall. She was taller and no longer seemed too frail to hurt a fly. "You have a secret, don't you? I want to know."

The elevator slowed and shuddered. Its doors hissed, about to open.

Lady thrust an arm between Monique and escape. "Tell me your name. It'll be the best thing that happens tonight." Hot breath mixed with cool air. Her eyes flashed starlight. "Are you Monique?"

Monique's eyes widened. "What?"

"You are." Lady slipped back and clapped excited hands. "You are!"

Monique broke for the open doors. The world was dark outside the elevator, but she couldn't stay here another minute.

A fist struck between her shoulders and sent her sprawling onto a hard rock floor.

"Don't run from me!" Lady snapped. Pebbles scattered from her encroaching footsteps. "Where's Gray? Ooh-ooh!"

Monique reached ahead. They were in a tunnel only a little taller than Lady. However large the shafts the Gray Maiden used to climb between the underground and the surface, she would be slowed here.

Lady planted a boot in the small of Monique's back. "Stop moving. I'm sorry for hurting you, but you're not making it easy. This is the Worm's will. Ooh-ooh!"

Despite the weight on her spine, Monique tried to crawl. She wouldn't let these people feed her to the empty place. She'd die in the dark first.

"Ooh?" The Gray Maiden's call sounded higher-pitched than usual, but no less terrible.

"She's here!" Lady shouted. "And now she's—" Her boasting snapped into a shriek.

The weight sailed off Monique's back. She scrabbled to her feet and took off into the dark tunnel. Her shoes banged hard against the ground, and every footstep echoed.

So did Lady's screams. Her calls to the Gray Maiden seemed to have summoned something else.

Monique didn't pause until she reached a curve in the tunnel. The elevator's light looked distant behind her. Lady looked even farther away, and she was shrinking beneath a storm of gray-garbed figures, their hands and feet glistening with silvery talons. They reminded Monique of the Gray Maiden, but closer to Monique's size and less stooped. Were there five? Six? They moved too quickly to count.

Talons slashed and shoved. Lady fell screaming into a black crevice in the wall, and it swallowed her, body and screams and all. The Gray Maiden-like creatures dove after her. Their clamor cut short under the sudden clank of the elevator. Someone was calling it to the surface.

A shrinking column of light gleamed off fresh blood on the rock floor. Strands of red hair floated down and clung to its wet surface. The elevator engine thrummed and the doors hissed shut, sealing the underground in total darkness.

8
SUNLESS

MONIQUE PRESSED A HAND TO the wall's rough slate and ambled deeper into the tunnel. The underground was quiet except for her gasping throat, each desperate breath sucking in chilly air. The way ahead was unseen and unknown, but there was no going back. Lady couldn't hurt her again—wonderful. Other things still could, especially where it was too dark to see.

Monique's scraping sneakers told her the path sloped downward. She almost felt used to descent. The world had been pushing Monique down for as long as she could remember, even before she left Flushing, and while at one time she'd thought Donna might pull her up, instead she'd only dragged Donna down.

And here, in the deepest place, Monique found monsters.

Maybe if her parents knew how far she'd fallen, they would at last regret having banished their only child.

Unlikely. That was her imagination preying on her thoughts with something more painful than monsters in the dark—the illusion that her parents could ever accept her.

Donna had tried to kill that particular dream. "Nothing we could ever change would've made a difference," she'd said. "If one of us was a man, our hearts would be different, and neither of us would love the other. And then your parents will want to meet my family, there's our age gap—even where we live in New York is different. Just as well we're queer like nobody's business and that they tossed the both of us aside in the first place. Get it done with that way." She had tittered and then stared at her hands, her eyes solemn. "How did we ever come from them?"

Monique couldn't answer then. She wouldn't have had an answer now had a phantom Donna stood beside her and promised to become real and leave this place if only Monique could solve that puzzle.

Faint bluish-green light outlined a curve in the tunnel ahead. Whatever things had killed Lady might see Monique if she kept going, but better to be in the light where they, too, might be visible. The air nipped her skin, and she tugged her scarves tighter around her neck. Her breath puffed out in cold clouds where the tunnel opened into a vast cavern.

Stalactites dripped from the ceiling with points coated in glowing fungus. City bus-sized mushrooms sprang from every wall. Their caps, bright with blue-white light, cast a black silhouette at the cavern's center. A building grew there with a surface sleek and glassy. Pointed spires curved from all sides, and their shafts reflected points of fungal light like stars across a night sky. Between the spires, a massive round center climbed toward the ceiling. The stalactites could have kissed it had they dripped any lower. It was a flower of a building, blooming for daylight that would never come.

The Sunless Palace.

Monique's path hugged the cavern wall a few paces before jutting into a narrow stone bridge that crossed the cavern. It stretched between two curling spires and ended at the palace's core. Wooden beams patched up gaps in the stone path. The Worm's people must not have trusted the Worm's will to keep them from falling. Monique started to laugh and then covered her mouth. Too much noise might bring the creatures that killed Lady.

Water dripped from the ceiling into an unseen pool, making frequent plinking sounds that echoed through the cavern.

Monique imagined that rain or melting snow had to flood the palace's base at times. She leaned over the side of the bridge to glimpse an underground lake and regretted it. The drop was far and, as with the spires, the water below reflected fungi-covered stalactite points to imitate bright stars in its surface. Falling here would feel like falling into the sky before the water's surface smashed every bone in Monique's body.

She turned ahead and followed the bridge. One spire eased past her and then another. She didn't stop to marvel at them. The palace beckoned.

Where the bridge ended, a tall, black, and doorless opening welcomed her. One wooden plank squeaked underfoot to announce her arrival. Gooseflesh coated her arms. Without pause, she crossed into the palace.

A dome stuck up from the center of the floor, as if the palace had been carved from dark, smooth stone around the top of another building. Slender windows glowed along the dome's sides. The hallway around it formed a ring. Doorways breached the walls, but each opened onto stairways leading down, and Monique wasn't ready to descend any deeper yet. She stuck her head through the nearest window.

The dome formed the cap of a three-tiered room. Glowing fungi plastered its walls, giving light to the high windows at Monique's level. At the middle tier, a stone balcony stuck out from the wall. Ornate stone railing decorated its lip, overlooking the lowest floor.

Sudden raucous laughter bounded through the palace. The lowest level was stuffed with things to see, but Monique couldn't discern floor from furniture yet. Shadows smeared the edge of her vision. White walls and glowing mushrooms must've scarred her sight; her eyes might never work right again. She was going blind, or just crying, or both.

The only thing she could see below was Donna Ashton, the source of the laughter.

Her dark lips parted in an expectant grin. "Mon Amour."

9
THE SHAPE OF NOTHING

MONIQUE CRANED HER NECK DEEPER through the window. Her shoulders would make a tight squeeze, but she could manage.

The fall was something else. From the dome, it was a straight drop, and even if she were to catch the balcony first, it hung too high above the rest of the room to make the fall any friendlier. On a good landing, she would break her leg; on a bad one, her spine.

And yet every muscle urged that she throw herself through the window and plummet into Donna's arms.

Donna wore a black business jacket, dress pants, white button-down shirt, and navy blue tie. Chin-length black hair circled a severe face and dark blue eyes, and silver hair ran from her temples and behind her ears. Her skin looked paler than usual, but she seemed clean and healthy, not turned skeletal by these past three months.

Monique probably looked gaunt, and her clothes unwashed. She felt suddenly embarrassed.

But Donna smiled like there wasn't any difference between

them. "I wondered when I'd see you again," she said, leaning back in a crude stone seat. Lumpy pillows cushioned behind and beneath her. "You weren't supposed to come that way. Who put you through there? How long has it been?"

Monique almost couldn't remember. The months between Donna's springtime disappearance when the shelter closed and their reunion underground now were no longer worth chronicling. "Too long," Monique said.

Donna's grin pushed narrow cheeks up against her eyes. Monique couldn't help a same smile.

If only they weren't still so far apart.

The shadows left the edge of Monique's gaze; she could now make out Donna's surroundings. Her stone seat sat between two others and faced three more on the opposite side of a long stone table. Tattered yellow books littered its surface, surrounded by silver cups, bowls, and utensils. One end of the table broke off into jagged stone. No seat remained there, not even debris.

Across at the table's head was the only empty seat, an ornate, brass-colored chair. Its back twisted into corkscrew spires and their tips merged in a point. It almost looked like a throne. Behind it, the wall shined midnight blue, same as in the ceremony room, only here someone had bored small holes into the surface and filled each with a glowing fungus to imitate a wall of shining stars.

Every other place at the table held a body.

Their heads lolled over the backs of their stone seats, faces hidden by featureless silver masks beneath their bare bony scalps. A fungus grew through their ribcages and glowed beneath their clothes. Nothing else seemed to hold their bones together. One wore suspenders and a white shirt; another wore a pinstripe suit, a bowler hat lying in its lap. Two skeletons wore blue uniforms that might have come from a Civil War reenactment, while the last wore dust-coated furs. A hefty axe jutted up beside this skeleton's chair, the blade wedged into the stone floor and carved with runes that Monique couldn't make out.

Donna didn't seem perturbed. She had been down here long enough to get used to these corpses. She looked to the wall of stars, the bodies around her, and at last tucked her grin away. "Go ahead," she said. "You must have a million questions."

Monique studied the room once more and grimaced. "Are you okay?"

Donna threw her head back and cackled. Hers was life-giving laughter, more precious than water. "I'm fine. They keep me taken care of."

"How do I get down there? How do I get you out?"

"Get me out?" Donna shook her head. "Didn't anyone explain?"

They had tried, but it was all a jumble of ghost histories and strange titles. At best, Corene had tried to give warning. Monique's stomach quivered, but not in hunger. An uncomfortable yet familiar sense of wrong leaned over her back.

"No one knows I'm down here," she said.

"You came alone. Of course you did." Donna shook her head again. "I can't leave yet. I haven't been dismissed." She waved one hand at the table of skeletons. "Why do you think my friends are still here?"

"But if you tell me the way down, I can—"

"I have not been dismissed!" Donna snapped.

Monique jerked back from the window. "It's okay," she whispered to herself. Donna had been abducted by a great gray demon and stuffed into an ugly stone room full of corpses underground. She was understandably stressed. Monique doubted she could sit there composed were she in Donna's place. More likely she'd have been clawing at every wall until her fingers fell off.

She stuck her head through the window again. Donna now pressed her back into the pillows. Monique would've liked to nestle beside her. She needed rest.

But they weren't free yet. "How do I get you dismissed?" Monique asked.

"That's the part that makes it so absolute," Donna said. "The Worm decides who is and isn't dismissed. It's not up to me."

Then they had already explained everything to her. The Worm, her marital part in their plan. She probably knew about the song and what it did to people.

"Dee, I won't let them take you again," Monique said.

Donna lolled her head against the back of her chair, the same posture as her skeletal companions. Her grin returned.

It was a mask of her usual humor, but it felt wrong here. "Silly me. I was projecting expectations on you, and that isn't fair. You haven't been down here; can't have seen the things I've seen."

"I've seen things." Monique just didn't want to believe them.

"Have you seen the illogical? The impossible? Then you might be at the beginning of knowing."

"I can understand things, Dee. I'm not a child." But Monique couldn't help feeling like one by having to say that. It was an old argument between them and too tired for this place.

Donna closed her eyes. "Tell your skin to reach for the air. Do you feel the Worm's absence?"

Monique closed her eyes too and tried to visualize the palace floorplan. Finding the door to the balcony below would take time, let alone the bottom floor where Donna sat. For all Monique knew, there were stairways leading to lower places than the bottom floor, the Worm's tunnels digging forever beneath the earth.

Cold fingers slipped into her thoughts. Her eyes flashed open and flickered to the ringed hall that surrounded the dome, searching for shadows with silvery talons. There was no one she could see.

"Have you seen the Gray Maiden?" Donna asked, eyes still shut. "Heard of the Broken King? When the Worm descended from the stars, he gave their people everything, but when he demanded a bride in return, they turned their backs on him. It was their last mistake. Their end gave the world an absence, and we filled it. And yet, pieces of them remain. Dead and alive, happened and never happened, the Worm sews contradictions, defies logic, and rebuilds reality into a stronger structure—his will. He willed us together, Monique. Imagine, all of time conspired so that you and I could fall in love. We won't make the old history's mistake. We'll do right by him, and for that he'll grant us the impossible. He'll fashion a world without hate."

Monique leaned into the room with her knees hooked to the window ledge. There was something here that she couldn't see. Or something not here. Every thought came too cold to make sense.

"Do you understand?" Donna asked.

Monique wanted to run. "Why would I understand?"

Donna's eyes flew open and glared at Monique. "He'll give a world that won't hate us for who we love and who we are. A world where we can transform and become, all time twisting so that it was always right, and you won't have lived that pain we put you through."

Monique focused on Donna instead of the throne, easier on her thoughts, harder on her heart. "I made a choice."

Donna pounded the table, rattling bowls and bones. "You shouldn't have had to! This shouldn't be the kind of world that put you through that sicko's hack job, all that agony, so you'd feel more like a woman. You were always, always my girl!"

Monique crossed her legs over old scars on instinct. She could hardly think anymore. "I don't want to talk about that."

"It's okay, Mon Amour." Donna reached up as if her arm could stretch to the window and slide a gentle finger along Monique's jaw. "I'll make everything better, I promise." She turned to the shining throne and its wall of stars. "Thanks to him."

The cold sensation crept down Monique's spine. She recognized the feeling now, from Freedom Tunnel, from the ceremony room. The empty place had always been an ever-present nothingness to her, or else she'd have named it something else. It was a space that convinced her and everyone else to move around it.

But here she saw it for the first time—the shape of a brass throne. It had sought her out and drained all joy from this reunion. Only its sinking cold fingers remained inside her. *You knew it all along,* the empty place seemed to say. *This is why the likes of you cannot enter. Table for one, reserved by a monster.*

"You feel it," Donna said. She stood from her seat and approached the throne. "The absence offers the Worm a place of purity in our world upon his return. He will fill this space, same as his children will fill his bride when she sits beside him." She reached for the throne's arm and then let her hand drop to her side. It was the empty place; no one could bring themselves to touch it. No one mortal, at least. "An echo of his will. This is the throne of the Worm."

Monique imagined Donna's belly swollen with worms. "I

want to leave!" she shouted. "You have to leave with me!"

"How many times do I have to tell you? I haven't been dismissed." Donna passed between the throne and the wall of stars, circling the stone table. "The people above take care of me. I'm brought food, drink, books, buckets, pads, conversation, newspaper. I'm not a prisoner. I'm waiting for him. And even if I wasn't—"

She stepped away from the table and toward one fungal-lit wall. A crease broke through the stone, a possible exit from the throne room. She almost reached it, and then her legs buckled. Her whole body pivoted in place and returned to the table, shoulders cringing, breath gasping in and out as if exhausted by taking those few steps.

As if she'd been repelled from entering the empty place. Gravity glued her to this room.

"Even if I wasn't, I can't defy the Worm's will," she said. "Do you see?"

Monique didn't only see, but she felt seen. The throne was staring at her. She focused hard on Donna to avoid looking at it.

But Donna wouldn't look back. She collapsed into her seat, the effort at escape having taken a toll. "We've all tried. They're still trying. We love the Worm, but sometimes we'd like to see the sunshine."

"We?" Monique asked.

Something clinked below. A rattling sound began from one side of Donna and then echoed around the table. Bones clacked against stone. Teeth scraped the backs of silver masks, trying to chew them off their faces.

Hell. That's what this place was; no palace at all.

Monique grasped the sides of the window, her nerves twisting through her limbs. "You have to get out."

Donna settled her head on the table. "We have not been dismissed."

"The door." Monique swallowed an angry scream. "How do I get to the damn door, Donna?"

Donna lazily aimed one finger at the wall of stars. "There's a door, Mon Amour." She no longer seemed composed. She was right about projecting expectations. Monique was just as guilty, seeing Donna as her assured, confident self. This throne room was breaking her, and she needed help.

There were stairs to that level and a door that led inside the throne room. Once Monique found it and took Donna into her arms, she'd snap out of this reverence for the Worm, and they could figure a way out together. If Monique couldn't find the door, she would find a rope, a ladder, anything to get Donna out.

Heavy doors scraped stone below, and a finger of blue light scratched across the balcony. Footsteps echoed, the familiar *click*, *click* of talons on a hard floor. The Gray Maiden, arriving at last.

"I have to go," Monique said. "But I promise I'll find you again."

Donna's drowsy voice slurred. "Not been dismissed."

"Just give me time."

"Mon Amour?"

Monique froze. She needed to run before the Gray Maiden stepped onto the balcony and looked up.

An odd smile carved a wobbly line across Donna's face. "There's nothing to fear."

Monique ducked back as a massive shadow crossed the balcony's edge. Direction didn't matter right now. She had to get far away from the Gray Maiden. She darted along the ring-shaped hallway and fled down the nearest flight of stairs.

She would come back as soon as possible, at the lowest level. All that mattered was getting Donna out of here before these people turned her into the bride of their god or another meal for the empty place, whichever was worse.

Whether she liked it or not.

"Ooh?"

The Gray Maiden's song chased Monique to the bottom of the steps and into a lengthy hallway. The floor and walls were sleek stone that made scraping noises at her touch. Narrow windows opened on the mushroom-lit cavern outside while wide black doorways offered paths deeper within the palace. Dust settled around scarcely visible footprints. The Sunless Palace's halls were traveled often but weren't well-maintained.

Monique took a left and hoped for the best. Her every step clacked against the hard floor and echoed through the hallway.

"Ooh?" Louder now. Something in the Gray Maiden's

whale song said she knew there was an intruder. *Click, click* steps rang from all directions.

Monique wasn't sure whether to expect one enormous billowing shape or several closer to her size. Every blind corner threatened to throw her into the Gray Maiden's path. The smaller creatures could come from anywhere. The talons that tore Lady apart could easily do the same to Monique.

Donna must've talked up their relationship to Lady and others when they came to feed her, and that was why Lady knew the name Monique. Monique had been right to hide it. Donna was confused, brainwashed, and probably thought she was doing the right thing by telling the Gray Maiden that someone was here. She would recover once Monique brought her to the surface.

What they would do after that was anyone's guess.

"Ooh," the Gray Maiden called. No longer a question, and closer.

Monique took softer steps, but those couldn't get her anywhere fast. She ducked through one of the black doorways and into a corner, where she curled into a ball. There were crates in this room—she could tell by the scant light that brushed their wooden corners—but their contents were a mystery and she wasn't going to check. She would become a statue, cold and lifeless as the palace itself. If she kept quiet and didn't move, the Gray Maiden wouldn't find her.

"Oo-oooh!" The Gray Maiden howled, long and loud. Each cry jammed Monique tighter into her corner, as if hunted by the sound itself.

After a few minutes, the cry called from farther away. The Gray Maiden was hunting, but not finding anything. There were too many footprints in the dust for her to track properly, and maybe she didn't even know enough to follow them. Her footsteps echoed through the palace halls. Monique had no way to tell how close they might be. Even if the Gray Maiden had reached another floor, those channels beside the elevator suggested she might climb tight passages where she could use all four limbs to help her. She might scale the palace's outer walls just as easily.

"Ooh."

The song sounded far away, but Monique didn't trust her ears. She'd been running and creeping and aching all night.

Her sense of the world felt frail. She couldn't tell how many hours had passed since she'd stepped into Freedom Tunnel. Was it dawn yet? Time did not exist in this place. Only Old Time.

Her strained and malnourished muscles had no strength for searching this hall and however many more halls she'd have to wander to find the throne room. Her limbs took on ten-ton weights, and her unhappy stomach swallowed the palace itself. If she couldn't have food, then she needed rest. She would wear out otherwise and be no good to Donna.

Better to play smart and patient. Monique had spent three months hoping to see Donna again. She wasn't going to screw this up now that she'd finally found her.

Distant singing trickled into the cavern and filled the Sunless Palace. The choir was at work again. When their notes swelled, Monique glanced around the gloomy room, expecting faces to appear behind derelict crates and across the dimly lit doorway. Lady, Israel, Bouchard, others.

There was no one here. Lady was dead, and the rest of the Worm's people still gathered in the music hall above. Did their song descend from the practice room? Or was this the score to another murder?

Music had better purpose than killing. Monique would've sung against them if not for the Gray Maiden's prowling. Subway buskers, used to fighting train horns and railway clatter for listening ears, would've drowned out the choir, no trouble. They understood music. Its purpose was to fill the soul, with no purity in the Worm's name, and instead littered with the taint of mortal desires. The choir's pure reverence left Monique's soul empty.

10
NIGHT

HOURS PASSED. THE SONG EBBED and flowed while the palace remained unchanging, the choir showing incredible stamina. Now and then, the Gray Maiden called from a distance, her echo's direction forever indiscernible, but eventually even she must've tired.

When the choir's song faded for the last time, a quiet settled into the room. It helped grow the darkness from every corner and invited Monique's imagination to run wild. The Gray Maiden's sickle claw cut at her thoughts. Old Time had grown a dead world underground where creeping monsters sliced people apart. Corpses jittered in a room not far away, where the Worm's throne gave shape and purpose to the empty place. What other nightmares awaited beneath Empire Music Hall?

Monique couldn't guess. Everything she'd encountered since setting foot in Freedom Tunnel tonight—yesterday?—was beyond her. She barely understood human anatomy, let alone the dead history of a world that never was.

And wouldn't Donna call that a good thing? The empty

place's purity offered an entryway for her Worm. Empty minds might do the same. She was one of them.

It was too much.

Tears brimmed in Monique's eyes. She shoved her jacket sleeve against her mouth not to sob. She wasn't allowed to cry in this place or something might hear and come for her. It was like Freedom Tunnel again, keeping the sounds of her misery from the empty place.

And the empty place was here, too. It would take sound just the same.

Her stomach lurched. Corene's candy bar was long gone down the music hall's plumbing. Now Monique's guts wanted every blueberry Pop-Tart that the surface had to offer. She would've liked not to wonder where her next meal was coming from for a change.

A deep, rattling breath slipped in and forced out. Sleep would be best. Monique laid her head on one arm, where she bundled the tails of her tangled scarves. She tried to focus on the fungal glow of the doorway and not the thick darkness that owned most of the room.

No good. She felt the empty place as if she still remained beside it in Freedom Tunnel. She might lie next door to the throne room, close enough to grab Donna if she only knew the way. At least now she had a shape for the cold unease. How far did the throne reach? Its emptiness might climb beyond Freedom Tunnel and reach a patch of Manhattan sidewalk that pedestrians dodged without knowing why. Planes likely set their courses around where its cold fingers reached into the sky. And how deep did it burrow? Through the Earth's core? Did it reach the far side of the world, where ships met disaster avoiding it, an unexplainable blip on the map?

A rumble ate through the walls and made Monique think of subway trains. She was too deep underground to feel the subway, but the sound reminded her that there was a world up there and she could return to it.

With or without Donna.

No, that was exhaustion talking. Monique couldn't just quit. Donna had been at her side that last fateful day with Doctor Sam. She had tried to warn Monique that he wasn't the way to go, that they'd get the money together again and do things right, but the surgery wasn't for Donna. She could only understand so much.

Monique had gone ahead with it for herself. It wasn't only wanting love with another person who everyone said you couldn't be with. It was wanting something deep in your heart, needing it, while everyone said you didn't, and always for their own reasons.

For all the love Donna poured into their relationship, she didn't know the feel of those unwanted hunks of flesh hanging between Monique's legs. Only Monique felt her intrusive penis stiffening and softening against her will, an invader between her thighs and yet part of her. She liked being short and round-faced, fine. But she still had to contend with pronounced brow, throat, shoulders, and a myriad of other details that she wanted to tear off her body. Donna once said that hating how she looked was a part of being a woman these days. That hadn't made Monique feel any better over how she couldn't sort out the chemicals in her blood. The operation was the best she could do. She'd just wanted to love this one thing about herself.

But she couldn't even have that.

She hadn't expected art from the good doctor. A pristine hospital and kindly staff who would care for her were the stuff of dreams. At the very least, the surgery could've turned out successful. Wealthier women got the bodies of their dreams. Why couldn't Monique change one thing and have it go right?

Calling Doctor Sam's work a hack job would've been a compliment. He wasn't terrible at cutting flesh, but reshaping it was beyond his power or concern. He'd expected to take a kidney as a bonus for a job poorly done; instead he got whatever injuries Donna had inflicted. Monique didn't need to know more. She had her own scars to worry about and couldn't waste concern on Doctor Sam's.

The genitalia she needed were not unfamiliar territory. She had kissed the sweet lips between Donna's thighs on a hundred nights and knew what they should look and feel like. They were not what Doctor Sam had left to her. She didn't know what remained inside, only the scars on the outside.

Donna had cut the emergency room stitches out herself and held Monique's hand each time she cried. She didn't regret the lost tissue, only screamed at a world that had put her in this position.

"You're alive, Mon Amour," Donna had said. "How many women meet a man like him and never scream again?"

It made a sort of sense. Much as Monique hated Doctor Sam for turning her medical dream into a nightmare of blood and scars, she was grateful to have survived. Once the pain became occasional and she could mostly urinate without shrieking to wake the dead, she found at least that small pride in her brutal pelvic landscape. Her soft flesh had faced steel in battle and lived to fight another day. She could still hold Donna's hand, feel warm fingers across her face, look into her dark eyes and smile.

Donna had stayed through all of it.

Until the day she disappeared, when the Gray Maiden and Worm's cult came along with giant hands and a celestial destiny.

Monique scratched defiant nails down one arm. "Don't quit, okay?" she whispered to herself. No, she wouldn't quit on Donna after finally having found her, brainwashed or not.

Then what about Donna's promise? A world without hate. A world where time twisted so that everything was always the way it should be. Lady had spoken of transformation.

Monique's fingers slid to her side and prodded the scar where Doctor Sam had gone after one kidney. They traveled downward, beneath the rim of her jeans, to the edge of deeper scars. At the Third Coming of the Worm, what would she become?

What Corene had said outside Empire Music Hall remained a shadow outside memory, but what she'd said while listening to Lady rang loud and clear—healing and harm could be a matter of perspective. Monique wondered what she'd harm for the sake of healing.

She didn't think she could harm anyone. That would be too much like Doctor Sam.

And too much like that damn Worm. He'd messed with Donna's head, and she'd accepted him as sovereign and god, supreme editor of the universe. Don't like the supercontinent? Break it down into bite-size chunks. Don't like the people who live there? Replace them. The Worm's people painted his chaos in their walls and sang his legends, but they were tales of a murderer from the stars.

And Donna was supposed to bear his cosmic children?

Absolutely not. They would escape together instead. She might bear psychological scars to match Monique's, her perspective distorted by emotional torture. Better that than withering into one more skeleton trapped in the throne room, her teeth scraping at the underside of a silver mask, never to leave the table.

Never dismissed.

Every wall blurred from sleek stone to dreamy fog to black tinted glass. Behind the glass, there walked shadow women, their legs bent backward and faces shrouded. They reminded Monique of the Gray Maiden-like creatures that had killed Lady. Monique couldn't hear them, but their hooting calls rattled through her bones. Their song filled the air, at first in greeting each other and then to shatter the glass that held them back.

They noticed Monique and turned to her. They quit groping at glass walls and somehow reached through them, grasping at her skin and clothes, eager to wear her instead of their shrouds and gowns. These faceless women craved faces.

Monique couldn't fight them off. She wasn't sure she should try.

She stirred awake. There was no glass here, only darkness, the smell of dust, and the sound of dripping water out in the cavern.

And a hand that reached for her shoulder. Not the cold nothing grasp of the empty place, but solid and clammy, its digits curling into cruel talons.

The shadow women were here. They had followed Monique through Empire Music Hall, down the channels past where they'd killed Lady, and out of Monique's dreams.

And they wanted her.

11

MIMIC

MONIQUE JAMMED HER FINGERS UP one jacket sleeve—empty. Dream's fog slipped back, and she remembered dropping her switchblade when the Gray Maiden had grabbed Corene. It was gone, but her hands couldn't seem to accept that.

Two of the creatures crawled down the walls, their thin gowns draped over backward-bent legs. Drooping hoods shrouded their faces. Unlike the Gray Maiden, their arms stretched bare from their trunks, the flesh dotted with feather-like bristles. They crept across stone in rigid, jerking movements, their talons scraping sparks in the air. At every flash, wild amber eyes shone in the dark.

Monique darted from her sleeping corner and into the palace hallway. Another figure slinked in the shadows to the right, driving Monique to spin around and slam her shoulder against a corner. Static tingling replaced her skin. She couldn't stop; the creatures' hands were already reaching for her through the doorway, she knew it. There wasn't time for gentleness.

She hurried left of the door. Far down the hallway, another shadowy figure crept down the wall between two fungal-lit windows. This one meant to cut her off.

A doorway opened in the wall opposite the windows, where a stairway drifted down. Monique took the steps two at a time and plowed into a larger hallway. The ceiling hung high overhead and indistinct symbols carved the walls. She didn't have time to inspect them for clues on reaching the throne room. Talons scraped in the stairwell behind her, urging her onward.

Yet another Monique-sized creature slipped through a window ahead. Her gown billowed around her feet, one slender sickle claw poking up from rumpled cloth. How many of them were there? The palace basement might have been full of sickle-clawed pests in place of New York's usual rats and spiders.

Monique didn't slow. If these creatures caught her, they might do to her what they had done to Lady. Blood glistening in elevator light would not look so different from blood glistening beneath luminous mushrooms.

A cool draft slipped through a tall glowing doorway beside the windows. Monique darted under its wide stone arch and out into the open underground cavern. A small patch of flat rock spread from the base of the palace and beneath the caps of enormous glowing mushrooms. It ended at the shore of a vast subterranean lake.

There was nowhere to hide between the exit and the shoreline. The air was so chilly that it drew out Monique's breath in wispy white puffs; the water had to be even colder.

Behind her, six creatures crept through the immense palace doorway, their shadowy gowns seeping from the darkness itself. Outside those dimly lit halls, their jerky, deliberate movements seemed eerie and dreamlike. Some crawled on the ground. Others walked on two birdy legs with their backs hunched like the Gray Maiden's.

Monique stumbled, tripped, and sprawled forward. She hadn't been watching where she was going and couldn't have seen any jutting rocks, tricky as distended sidewalk squares. Her knee slammed into the ground beside a mushroom's stiff stalk. Every joint screamed.

"Ooh?" The hoot was higher and flatter than the Gray

Maiden's.

A dark shape slinked alongside her on all fours. Monique could hardly make out the eyes anymore, only the vague movement of a head and limbs within the hooded gown. The creature pressed one knee hard against the ground, mimicking Monique's position.

"Ooh?"

Monique reached ahead, trying to crawl away. The water had to be freezing, but maybe they would hate it more than she would.

The creature reached the same arm ahead. "Ooh?" Another two creatures crept behind the first. The rest shuffled closer, their sickle claws prodding at hard earth and upturning small stones. Their talons closed in around Monique's face and limbs.

She froze mid-crawl. The creatures might as well have held her switchblade to her throat.

A hand slid up the back of her jacket, cold and clammy. Another hand pawed at her neck, its talons tearing threads from one of her scarves. The creatures patted at her shoulders, legs, arms, hair. One drew damp fingers down her face, their talon tips teasing at the corners of her eyes, the edges of her nose, past her round cheeks and soft chin. Another creature's talons snagged Monique's beanie and tugged it off, exposing her hated brow. She almost snatched it back on instinct, but she remembered Lady's shrieks and the quiet that came after they were cut short. One wrong move could turn these creatures from curious to lethal.

Their pawing became desperate, insistent. "Ooh?" the first one cried, and the others echoed. "Ooh? Ooh?" As if they needed to ask a question but didn't have the words.

At last, one hand fell away. The others slid off, some reluctant. One set of talons dragged faint scratches down Monique's jacket sleeve and pierced the denim, leaving crosshatches to the marks she'd made herself. She tried not to flinch. Their gowns slid past her, the creatures crawling and shuffling toward the lake. They became indistinct, a great mass of flowing garments and bristly limbs.

The first one who'd mimicked her remained at her side, waiting. "Ooh."

When Monique stood shakily, so did the creature. They

came to about the same height. Monique tilted her head and watched the creature do the same, mimicking every movement.

"Ooh?" Mimic asked.

Monique nodded. "Ooh," she said. She had to still be dreaming.

At her first step, her knee cried out and began to sag. She tensed her thigh muscles and pressed the other leg hard into the ground for balance. If she fell, so would Mimic. Monique had a responsibility now.

She swallowed a laugh. Given time, she would end up haunting this place too, another lost creature doomed to crawl through palace halls and call "Ooh" into the darkness. If she gave in and became part of this place, at least then she could sleep. Maybe her terrible hunger would subside.

Her next step felt stronger than the first, and walking became easier after that, her knee no longer caring that it ached. Mimic stuck to her side, only stepping when she did. Mimic's sickle claws breached the bottom of her gown, but they didn't feel like weapons now, only parts of her body. Her sister-creatures led on.

Monique wasn't certain about following them, but they kept looking back. She was expected. She and Mimic followed toward the water.

The lake was not empty. Its shoreline narrowed to a slick stone bridge rising scant inches from the water's surface. Mimic's sister-creatures grasped its sides as they crept out onto the still water. Their drooping gowns dragged at the surface, wetting the hems.

At the bridge's end, an indistinct structure climbed from the water. The cavern's eerie light reflected across its surface, painting the illusion of a night sky. The water reflected the structure, and its black glass surface reflected that reflection, two warped mirrors held too close together and distorting all clear perception of the structure's design. It was a pyramid. It was an inverted pyramid. It was something of a sphere, too. And yet it seemed to have no absolute shape, its curling arms reaching in all directions. For all Monique knew, in daylight it would have looked as square-shaped and mundane as her old apartment building.

But this was the underground, where reality twisted to the

Worm's will.

Monique stepped onto the bridge, Mimic at her side. Water dripped from the ceiling and into the lake; nothing else disturbed the surface.

The other creatures slinked up to the black glass structure. Their reflections cast and multiplied a thousand times across its surface before a tall doorway swallowed them. An odd scent breathed from the opening in their place. Monique had never smelled anything like it before. Not unpleasant, but unnatural in ways she couldn't understand, like bathing a newborn baby in embalming chemicals. The wrong mix of life and death.

Mimic's head craned toward the structure, eager to follow her sister-creatures yet unwilling to abandon Monique.

Their footsteps fell muffled on the black glass. Monique's face appeared briefly across every surface, and it was strange seeing herself without her red beanie. One of the creatures had to have stuffed it inside her gown. Monique had a feeling she'd never wear it again.

Her reflections vanished as she and Mimic crossed the threshold of the black glass doorway. The structure was either built as a single room or split into a million, the insides more complex than any hall of mirrors. Mimic's sister-creatures melted into their reflections, the five of them replicating across glass until gowns, limbs, and talons echoed over every surface. Gnarled pillars jutted ten feet off the floor, each a blend of black glass and stone.

A throat cleared. It didn't sound like the creatures' shrunken hoots and didn't come from where they crawled on the walls. The sound came from the room's center. "Shouldn't you be piercing the universe?" a dry voice asked.

Someone sat up from the floor and lifted her head to meet Monique's gaze.

Corene.

12
THE CHAMBER OF OLD TIME

MONIQUE STOMPED ACROSS THE BLACK glass floor, a stunned smile on her lips. Everyone who had been brought below was alive. Maybe she could get her hopes up for a change.

"Not so loud," Corene hissed. She clawed at her hair, her once-red nails now black and broken. She sat upright on the floor and yet couldn't seem to stand. Black glass grasped up her clothes. "We're not safe."

Shadows crossed her face as two of Mimic's sister-creatures slinked across the entrance. Now that they had led Monique here, it seemed no one was allowed to leave. One creature stretched her arm, pointing to one side of the room. Mimic raised hers, too.

Monique followed their fingers and noticed a large lump that rested against a broken stone pillar. Sickle claws poked from enormous curled feet.

The Gray Maiden.

"What's she doing here?" Monique asked.

"She sleeps here," Corene said. She chuckled hoarsely, her

throat rumbling with gravel. "Welcome to the Worm's gar-bage can, the Chamber of Old Time."

Had someone mentioned that name before? Monique thought Lady might have. Too many titles and monikers now mixed into a dreamy syllable stew.

Corene craned her neck. "Where'd your red cap go?"

Monique brushed a hand over her forehead but couldn't hold it there. She wanted her red beanie back, anything to hide her upper face and help her look more like herself. There was hardly anyone to see her, but that didn't matter. She felt ex-posed as Corene's gaze crawled over her from head to toe. Careful thoughts weighed so heavily in Corene's expression that Monique could almost hear them. *I thought you were a girl. You sound like a girl. How old are you really? You're a what?*

But Corene didn't say any of those things. She deflated into her clothes. "I wish I had time to know you better."

"You do. You will." Monique stepped closer and then stopped.

Mimic no longer walked by her side. She looked to Monique, and then Corene, and didn't move. Something was wrong. All Monique wanted right now was to throw her arms around Corene's neck and help pull her out of this hellhole, but she should've been able to leave on her own power then.

Monique slipped back to Mimic and stared at Corene. "What's wrong? Why can't you run?"

"Because the Worm's people want me to transform. To transcend." Corene rolled up one jacket sleeve. Chunks of her arm seemed missing, and in their place spread the same black glass sinew that ate through stone and formed the chamber's walls. The same reflective infection spread over Corene's feet, legs, and hips, forming stiff strands that chained her to the floor. "I know what you're thinking, and yes, it's contagious. Old Time is working its wonders on me. Spend a while here and the universe can't be sure where you belong anymore."

"I thought you were dead." It blurted out quicker than Monique could stop it.

"You'll think right, soon." Corene scratched at the glass in her arm, making it squeak. Did her skin still itch underneath? She nodded toward the Gray Maiden, whose heavy breath chugged in and out. "If she catches you, she'll keep you. Hell won't suffer saints to reach for sinners."

Monique rubbed at her aching shoulder and watched Mimic do the same out of the corner of her eye. "Don't quit on me."

"Quitting isn't a crime." Corene sank into her captive nest. "We quit things all the time for our own good. I quit smoking, remember?"

Monique couldn't help a half-giggle. Corene was pulling the same bright-side-of-life nonsense as Donna when moving out of Marigold & Cohen or while Monique was healing after Doctor Sam, and Monique was falling for it. Cursed with affection for older women, it seemed. She thought some Freud-type might analyze that to hell and back about her mother. She didn't care.

"You must've quit a bad relationship before, yes?" Corene asked. "Sometimes you can't find the right thing unless you quit the wrong one. Isn't that what you did? Whoever anyone thought you were before, you quit it. I don't know your name, but I bet you don't call yourself what they used to call you. You quit that, too, and now there's light in your eyes that wasn't there before, was it?"

"I don't want to talk about this," Monique said, but she couldn't help thinking about it. Leaving her parents' home hadn't been her choice, but she'd put her foot down and meant it. She was Monique, no matter who they thought she might be. But did quitting the past mean she should quit just anything? Donna? Her life? The universe?

She nodded toward Mimic and then the sister-creatures on the walls. "Maybe they know how to get you out?"

"Ooh," Mimic said.

"I don't think they understand," Corene said. "Our entire existence spawned from the afterbirth of their apocalypse. Why help us?" Dark tears formed in her eyes, dotted with black glass and blood. "Once there was a worm that dreamed it was a god. I wonder what kind of people they might've been if not for him. They gave up their own future, beautiful or horrific, and instead built the Great Pangaea Kingdoms to worship him. Then their kings refused to sacrifice a daughter as his bride, and doom came for them all. Old Time seeps through that stab wound in the universe. It hasn't finished one death and now it's started another."

"I think death is what happens when anyone meets a god."

Monique realized her feet were inching toward Corene's nest. The room blurred in and out, its reflections dancing and fusing. "I found Donna. They're going to make her the Bride of the Worm. Do you know the way to the throne room?"

"Will it matter?" Corene asked. "No one below ground has been dismissed, so said our friend Lady."

Monique clenched her teeth not to scream. "Well, Lady's dead, and I'm sick of hearing that word!" She glanced wide-eyed in the Gray Maiden's direction, but the monster was still asleep. Monique softened her voice. "There has to be a way."

"The key is determinism. Que sera sera."

"I'm not quitting."

"That's not what I mean, you lovesick, stubborn girl." Corene sighed hard; breathing seemed a challenge. "It was around this equivalent year in Old Time that the old kings upset the Worm. For our world, it's been a 175-million-year crawl since he reached back and smashed the supercontinent to get to this point again. But he doesn't have to do that. He's coming to a determined point in time and space, whenever he's offered a bride and his people sing the song that pierces the universe. Is Donna the bride in that moment? If so, you'll fail, and the Worm will take her. If she isn't, maybe you'll rescue her, and the Worm cult will carry on searching until they find the true bride. We can't know the determined moment. It might be hundreds of years from now. Fate is a tapestry of impossible questions with unimaginable answers."

Monique smiled over Corene. "If it was fate, he would've had a bride on the first try."

Black glass flecked Corene's lips. "I'd like that. But what if the Worm always meant to test the old kings, have his godly tantrum, and destroy their history so that we could rise from early mammals instead? The Worm is absolute, but he's not picky about leaving ruin wherever he goes."

"No, I think he likes it. Donna acts like he's made an example of Old Time—humans, stay in line or you'll end up like *them.*"

Two of Mimic's sister-creatures crawled at the edge of Monique's sight, their gowns merging with shadow. The other three crept along the walls. They didn't belong, these creatures with birdlike legs, sickle claws, and whale cries. They wore clothes like humans, but made from what, silkworm silk? Or some animal that had only existed in their dead timeline?

"He who cleaves time in two leaves a half-divided history." Corene pointed over her shoulder at a pillar in the back of the chamber. "I found a king of their time here. The King of the Broken Throne, split and punished between timelines."

Monique looked to the Gray Maiden again and kept her distance as she circled Corene. "The one they love. Here?"

"In a fashion. Love is a strong word."

Monique crept toward the pillar, Mimic slinking beside her. This was the lair of the Broken King who had brought the Worm down on two histories, founder of the nightly ceremony, the seer who sounded so great in Bouchard's speech and Lady's rambling.

But Donna was right; there was nothing to fear. The King of the Broken Throne didn't rule the underground. What remained was neither messiah nor demagogue.

Deep in the chamber stood a shard of blasted wall where a standing body had long ago fused with stone. Sinewy black glass spread root-like from its every extremity. A fleshless skull turned upward with the snout frozen open in an eternal scream. The limbs bent backward, so overcome with glassy strands that Monique couldn't tell their exact shape. The abdomen was a petrified broken sack. Something had been torn loose.

"Oo-ooh," Mimic sang, her notes long and discordant.

Monique didn't think guts alone had gone missing from the Broken King's middle. "The King of the Broken Throne was a mother?" she asked.

"I was surprised, too," Corene said. "But the Great Pangaea Kingdoms had their own society and the people upstairs make a habit of getting things wrong. We glued the word king to men. Their kind's equivalent must've spanned genders. She was the seer, after all, so she set the precedent. I wonder how many years her kingdoms lasted between the First Coming and their end." Her shoulders slumped, the floor dragging at her. "She was the first to meet the Worm and look what he did to her."

Monique reached for the torn belly and then let her hand drop. Mimic did the same. To touch would not be right. "She doomed Old Time."

"She doomed herself and her child." Corene halfway turned, trying to face Monique. Every movement made her wince. "According to the cult's myths, at the Second Coming of the Worm, he demanded one of the old kings offer their daughter as bride. They didn't say, 'No.' They hesitated, each hoping one of the others would speak up first. The Worm had expected them to jump at the chance, but they loved their daughters too much to let any of them become a vessel for the Worm's offspring. In their moment's pause, he was already reaching back in time. But he looked to her, the seer who became king, who was with child, and thought she might promise her unborn daughter to him. How could she love someone she hadn't even met? And yet she refused." Corene pointed at the corner. "She already loved her daughter too much."

Her finger aimed at the sleeping Gray Maiden.

"The Worm took her," Monique said. Revulsion surged up her insides.

"He shattered the seer's seat—King of the Broken Throne—and left her daughter to grow in an unwelcoming timeline." Corene clicked her tongue as if admonishing a misbehaving student.

"How do you know all this?"

"He told me." Corene slumped deep into herself. She seemed not to want to look, but her head couldn't help turning to one side. "I found who I was looking for, too."

Monique glanced over but didn't approach. The floor bulged into a jagged lump. She could believe its glassy spines were once the scraggly beard of Professor Abraham Clarke, now sharpened and hardened by Old Time.

"Corene, I'm so sorry," Monique said.

"He was still alive when the Gray Maiden put me down here. He was raving. I gleaned what I could. He was desperate to live by then, his thoughts torn apart, our every physics theory disintegrated by dogma. Now I'm the only one who understands." Leaning her head back, Corene bared her throat as if ready for Monique to cut it. "I wonder if I'll worship the Worm by the end."

The chamber's doorway cleared of shadows. Monique had apparently seen what the creatures meant for her to see, but now she didn't want to leave. They slinked along the walls, flesh against reflection.

"Ooh?" Mimic asked.

Monique reached for Mimic's face and felt beneath her hood. Her skin was cold and clammy. Soft spines coated her neck, what Monique imagined a hedgehog must've felt like when stroked head to tail. "How did you get here?" she asked.

"Ooh." Mimic reached for Monique's face and laid a cool hand against her cheek. Talons dug into her oily hair.

"I think they seeped from Old Time, same as the palace," Corene said. "And Old Time seeped from the Broken King. This chamber seems an accident, huh? Maybe the Worm meant things to turn out this way, maybe not. The machinations of we small things are beneath his mighty gaze. We might scurry unimpeded. We might plot."

"Even the Worm might make a mistake then." Monique lowered her hand from Mimic's face and stepped toward Corene. Her shoulders weighed too much suddenly, as if she had taken on the guilt of this room. "But everyone's still afraid of him."

"Fear is a symptom. It happens when our old perspective breaks down." Corene stared hard into Monique's eyes. "Sometimes we have to break down to see things in new ways."

"Did Abraham teach you that?"

"I taught myself that. And now I'm teaching you." Corene's chest heaved in and out. Old Time was invading her organs and killing her, same as Abraham. "Imagine synchronized wormholes across multiple star systems. The space circumvented by wormholes can only be a worm."

Monique knelt beside the black glass nest. The chamber's wrong scent came strongest here, mixed with unwashed skin and beleaguered regret. "What are you saying?" she asked.

"That kind of vast celestial movement might twist gravity and flip magnetism." Corene raked her hair again. Patches of black glass glistened across her scalp. "A black hole is so dense that it can crush time itself. Why can't a wormhole? And so, Abraham and I theorized that some cosmic cataclysm beyond our understanding once tore through multiple wormholes and spilled over Earth, striking present and past, shifting tectonic plates—the planet's history was forever altered. Old Time is the seepage from a parallel present. What we've discovered is not the will of any deity, but the echoes of a chronologically erased culture, its pieces leaking into our universe. They paid fealty to that cosmic movement, but the cosmos has no mercy."

"Do you know about the people in the throne room?" Monique asked, desperate. "They're dead and alive."

"If there is such a thing as a soul, why wouldn't it be governed by the same natural forces as everything else? They sink into the gravity well. That's what we theorized anyway." An uneven smile split Corene's face. "I bet Abraham told them as much once he heard out their mythology. He was never tricky like you and me. No one liked that, I'm sure, so they let the Gray Maiden drag him down here. All for a little starlight."

Monique couldn't be certain that Corene was right, but she didn't know enough about the stars to say she was wrong. All these people with their songs and murder might as well be bowing to Jupiter's eye or Saturn's rings. The Worm might be an imagined god, a cosmic power same as gravity or a supernova, but no consciousness. No will.

Only an empty place.

Whether he was a god or gravity, this place, these people, had taken those who were desperate or brilliant or both and turned them into single-minded zealots. They had done the same to Donna and Abraham. Corene saw it in her future. They would do it to Monique, too, given the chance.

She turned to Mimic, just one bystander beneath celestial calamity. "I wish I knew what you knew."

Mimic said nothing.

"I bet you'd tell me it'll be okay. You'd tell me no one should worship this power. But really, I'm just pinning my thoughts to you, like my parents did to me because I was a quiet kid. You can't tell me anything, and that isn't any fair."

To entirely erase Old Time would've been kinder than casting its fragments to wander lost in an alien world. Time that never was, sliced from its source by the Worm's carelessness. There shouldn't have been a cataclysm that left echoes caught here, forever repeating. The underground was not a city, but a mass grave, its ghosts forever buried, its ghouls so desperate for a place to belong that they put their hopes of salvation in a worm of uncaring stars, as eternal and thoughtless as the empty space between them.

Donna was wrong. There was everything to fear.

"I have to help Donna," Monique said. She reached for Corene. "But I can't leave you like this."

"I can't follow." Corene's legs fidgeted, caught in black glass teeth. "Seems the people upstairs were right about one thing—the Worm's will is absolute."

"The Worm makes mistakes. If Old Time was shoved through because he couldn't care less, I can grab Donna by the arm and yank her out, dismissed or not. And I can rip you out of this, too." Monique offered an open hand.

"Don't." Corene lowered her head to the floor. "This shit will spread into you, and you'll die like Abraham. You'll never save Donna. Wouldn't that be too much like quitting for you?"

Monique's thoughts rolled beneath the weight of everything Corene had said about stars, wormholes, and gravity, about quitting and retaking and transcending. The only word to come out was, "Sorry."

"We'd tear the universe apart for the people we love, but sometimes we forget to love ourselves. It's not your fault, kid."

"Monique."

Corene forced a smirk. "You tear them down, Monique. Run with Donna and break everything in your way."

Monique didn't leave yet. She drifted toward the slab where the Broken King seeped not a dead history, but physical sorrow. No one escaped the Worm, it seemed. A survivor, smarter than most, Donna had accepted that and allowed the Worm to break her. Now she flowed with his will.

But Monique couldn't.

She reached for the Broken King's skull and ran her fingers down a glassy face. Black teeth reflected her fingertips. "Sorry," she said again. She thought of her scars, small to the scars of Old Time, and wondered if the Broken King was like her, afflicted with anatomy that didn't match the truth inside. There was no knowing. The culture of the Great Pangaea Kingdoms couldn't be explained by an altar to its loss.

"Ooh," Mimic added.

It wasn't much of a eulogy for a dead mother, a Broken King, or a wronged universe, but it would have to do.

As Monique stepped back from the pillar, her heel faltered on an uneven surface, some obstruction. She heard a familiar click and felt a sharp blade jab through the sole of her shoe, into the pad of her foot. A scream tore up her throat before she could snap her lips shut.

Talons scraped black glass. Something large gasped, awakening.

What had she stepped on? She lifted her leg and her fingertips crossed a plastic handle and trigger—her own switchblade. The Gray Maiden had taken it after all, curious as her fellow refugees. Blood coated Monique's fingertips.

A shadowy bulk rose against a separate pillar, and her sickle claws tapped the floor. "Ooh?" The questioning whale song came deep and tired. The Gray Maiden was still groggy.

Monique spun around, stumbled, fell on the glass, and scrabbled up. A pointless accident, easily avoided. The Gray Maiden was moving. There would be no evading her this time; Monique was bleeding everywhere. Mimic no longer walked by her side. She had dipped into the shadows with her sister-creatures. They might've been afraid of the Gray Maiden too, so much larger than the rest of them.

Monique limped past Corene and toward the chamber doorway. Heavy steps thudded behind her. *Click, click.*

"Don't hurt her!" Corene shouted. She clutched at the Gray Maiden's cloak and tangled it around her arms. Black glass thorns snagged the fabric. "Leave her alone; she's just a kid!" Her eyes flashed wide at Monique. "Run like hell!"

Monique twisted on her good foot and stumbled out of the chamber. A wail rang across black glass, so harsh that it might pierce the universe. It throttled her nerves, but she couldn't let it stop her from leaving or else Corene would die for nothing. She had to get back across the bridge.

Back to Donna.

13
BLOOD AND STONE

THE PALACE HALLS FELT DARKER than before, but Monique couldn't stand in the palace entrance waiting for her eyes to adjust. The Gray Maiden wouldn't be long.

Corene didn't deserve this. Old Time was grave enough for an entire people. Hadn't it consumed enough lives? Monique guessed not. She would be next if she didn't hurry.

She took a blind turn and hobbled down the sleek stone hallway, her blood-slick shoe squeaking with each step. Windows glowed to one side; doorways stood dark to the other. She kept watch for any passageways that might lead toward the palace center, throne room, Donna—all the important beats.

"Ooh!" A blaring hoot rang from outside. The Gray Maiden had finished with Corene. It would take her only moments to notice the blood trail leading over the lake's bridge and inside the palace.

And what could Monique do about it? Every other footstep shot screams up her leg, and her switchblade felt pathetic in her fist. Head spinning, she stumbled down the hall and slammed her shoulder into a corner. The Gray Maiden would catch up at this rate. She knew her way, and no one had slowed her down with a stab wound to the sole.

"OOH!" She was here.

Monique eyed the floor. Couldn't she lie down and let everything just happen?

No, that would be quitting. This was a new floor for her, and Mimic and her sister-creatures weren't here to bar the way. Monique had free reign to find the throne room so long as she was quick. Once she held Donna in her arms, they could break for the elevator, and soon after that, they would escape. Monique hobbled onward.

"—and when you're wondering why the Worm needs kings, it'd be like if we put you in charge of running an ant-hill."

Voices filled the hall before Monique could slow down. Flashlights slashed through the black corridor. Three young men walked the palace halls, one carrying a bucket while the other two carried crates.

"You'd be too big," one of the crate carriers went on. "Same with the Worm. A god who cracks land would hurt—who are you?"

Monique hadn't realized there would be other people in the palace halls. She studied them. They were in their mid-twenties and looked sturdy, but none of them were armed and they had their hands full.

She raised her switchblade and stamped toward them. "Out of my way!"

The men didn't argue. Their bucket sloshed and crates thumped as they strafed aside. She darted past, down the hall.

"But we just did throne room duty," one of them said, as if Monique had been sent to help them.

She didn't answer. All that mattered was grabbing Donna and getting her to the surface. Back on the street, they would be safe if there was daylight. No way the Gray Maiden would come out while the sun shined and reveal herself to the world. They could make it to Jersey long before sunset and just keep running, hitchhiking, anything to get as far from the city as humanly possible. Across the country, trading Atlantic Ocean for Pacific, maybe they'd find peace where the Worm's will couldn't touch them. Monique had never seen the west coast.

She'd scarcely left the city.

"OOH-OOH!" The Gray Maiden's foghorn cry swelled to deafening.

Monique pounded the floor, half-limping, half-jogging. There was a turn ahead, one that might take her closer to the palace's center.

Footsteps clacked behind her as the men made to follow. One of them started to say something and then his voice cracked into a scream. Monique caught a flailing flashlight beam out of the corner of her eye as she made the turn.

The screamer writhed between the Gray Maiden's fingers. He could no better escape her than anyone else. Her shoulders hunched around her head, higher than usual, and her trembling limbs lit the air with hot rage. She lowered the man, as if starting to put him down, and then thrashed at the ceiling, smearing his skull across black stone. She then reeled back and threw him down the hall.

Monique ducked just as his body hurtled past her, sending an airy gust through her hair. It struck the wall and seemed to pop. Raw fluid spat over slick stone and its residue sprayed Monique's jeans and shoes.

The Gray Maiden didn't need to do that, but the man had been in her way, and that was all the reason she had needed to crush him. And it was easy.

Monique couldn't afford to slow again. She stomped away from the forming puddle. Its crimson streaks crept after her down the next hall and into the palace's shadows.

The hall curved ahead, forming a hook toward the palace's center. At the inside of its curve, Monique crossed a set of iron double doors, scarcely visible in what light still ebbed from the outer halls.

"Please be right," she whispered, and pressed at the doors. They were heavy, but each gave under her hands. Their whining creak echoed through the corridors. "Please, please." She limped through and shoved them shut behind her.

Glowing fungi matted the walls of a three-tiered room and lit the ornate stone railing of its balcony. Dark, slender windows glowered from the domed ceiling above. A familiar stone table stretched across the floor below.

The throne room. Monique was still a level too high, but she was here. That would have to be enough.

An open book sat in front of Donna's place at the table, but she wasn't reading it. She stared at the wall of fungal stars and the brass throne seated beneath it.

Cold fingers of the empty place clawed at Monique's skin. It had been waiting for her return. It would have to wait forever after this; she was never coming back here. She wouldn't even glance at Freedom Tunnel.

Donna turned to the balcony. "There you are."

"Climb onto the table," Monique said. She laid her middle across the balcony railing and outstretched one arm into the room. "Jump and grab my hand. I'll pull you up."

Donna closed her book and sighed. "Monique, I've told you. I haven't been dis—"

"I'm sick of hearing that!" Monique leaned deeper. The ache in her shoulder said Donna's weight might tug her arm from its socket, but she didn't care; she had another. "Everything you know about the Worm is bullshit. And even if he was a god, you don't have to do what he wants."

"And what about what I want?" Donna stood from her stone seat and glared past Monique's hand, into her eyes. "We shouldn't have to crawl beneath this world any longer. He can give us a world without hate. He can heal you."

"He's not a healer."

"We're not the only ones." Donna paced the length of the table, eyeing her dead tablemates. "Everyone who's different, everyone who needs a path out from under society's bootheel—the Worm will carve that path."

Monique noticed she'd withdrawn her arm without meaning to, as if her hand were repulsed by Donna's devotion to the Worm. Never mind that; Donna wasn't herself right now.

Monique reached again. "This isn't how we fix the world," she said. "I know more than anyone that patience is slow and soul-breaking, but it's better than rushing to Doctor Sam. I don't know if the Worm is a god or physics gone wonky, but all he's ever done is destroy. He found a world of one people and carved their land into kingdoms. When they didn't do what he wanted, he carved their world itself, and we picked up the pieces. All he does is carve, Donna. The Worm is Doctor Sam for the universe."

Donna shuddered—a genuine reaction. She'd been at Monique's side, changing bandages, wiping pus from wounds, helping her remember to walk again. They couldn't share pain in their bodies, but Donna had absorbed some of it into her soul.

Monique pushed through. "Now we're the world's people instead. He's not going to save or heal. He didn't help anyone last time he carved everything. He won't help anyone now. I don't know where the right carving or healing might ever come from, but it's not from him."

Donna lowered her head. Her shoulders were shaking.

Monique stretched over the railing on tiptoes, far as she could without falling, and reached down. Her injured foot pleaded for her to come back. "Grab my hand."

"It won't work," Donna said, her voice flat.

"It'll work because I'm helping you! You're not alone. He'll try to keep you. You'll take my hand, and I'll take yours, and you'll scratch and bite and flail around, try to break yourself in a fall so you won't have to leave that room, but no matter what, I won't let go. I'm your girl, remember? And you're mine. I won't let him make you his bride."

Donna looked up, her face perplexed, but there was light in her eyes.

"Please, Donna, take my goddamn hand!"

"Mon Amour, what are you talking about? This is the throne room." Donna waved at her skeletal tablemates. "These are the new kings. And so am I."

Monique stomach growled at being squashed against the railing. She ignored it. "But you're a—" The Broken King's torn belly dripped across Monique's mind. Both a king and a mother. "A woman." It didn't matter, she realized.

"In the Great Pangaea Kingdoms, king was a title that crossed all boundaries," Donna said, echoing Corene. "A new day arrives, the Third Coming of the Worm. The world will learn of King Donna, her power and reach, how she brings her love close and holds her tight." She looked up at Monique. "To keep her for destiny's sake."

Enormous hands seized Monique's sides and hauled her off the balcony railing into mid-air. She squirmed, but there was no getting loose.

The Gray Maiden raised her arms. "OOH!" Her breath gusted against Monique's back.

"Don't do this!" Monique shouted to the Gray Maiden.

"We're the same. It wasn't fair what the Worm did to you, and I get it, okay? I know what it's like to grow up wrong. And you didn't even get to pick your own name; everyone keeps deciding new ones for you. I know what you're going through!"

The Gray Maiden didn't react. She held too much pain inside her to care.

Monique snapped at her switchblade's trigger and drove the blade down at the Gray Maiden's fingers. It scratched across skin. The Gray Maiden squeezed, one thumb jamming into Monique's spine. Pain surged through her shoulders and down her arms. Her switchblade clattered on the balcony floor.

"Don't hurt her!" Donna shouted. She stood before the wall of stars, her suit both sickening and resplendent in the eerie fungal light. "Just keep her still."

The Gray Maiden's grip tightened, but no talons pierced Monique's skin.

She was too worn out to struggle. Her chest ached beneath giant fingers. Constriction and unconsciousness were coming, same as had happened to Phoebe and Corene and anyone else the Gray Maiden had grabbed.

Monique turned weary eyes down at the throne room. "You tell her what to do?" she asked.

"I tell everyone what to do," Donna said. "The Worm works through kings. Who do you think told them about you? Sent the Gray Maiden looking for you?"

Another wave of dizziness swept Monique's head. "But why?"

"Because I'm not the Bride of the Worm." Donna smiled brightly. "You are."

14
ALL OF TIME CONSPIRED

MINUTES, HOURS, YEARS—THEY SEEMED the same. Time had no meaning when there was no sun to revolve around, only a dark underground that spanned all existence. Monique would never see sunlight again.

Only the stars.

The Gray Maiden carried her through corridors and into a chamber where Monique was expected. Hands pawed at her from all sides. She would've preferred the touch of Mimic and the rest of the old kings' daughters, but these were talon-free human hands. They wielded scissors and brushes, rags and soap. They pulled off her jacket and shoes, and then they cut away her shirt and jeans. One sock came off hard, the foot caked in blood. Her scarves fell loose, exposing her throat.

She knew she was naked in the distant, impersonal way that she knew the sun would die someday. These were strangers. They could see her scars. She didn't want them to see, but there was nothing she could do about it. This hardly felt like her body now. It was theirs, and they would make it clean. Warm water ran through her hair, down her back, and into unseen drains. She heard the ringing of drops against stone. Hands scrubbed sweat from her skin and grime from beneath her fingernails. Knots fell, cut loose from her hair.

When the washing finished, her handlers bandaged her foot and dressed her in a silken gown that puddled at her feet. She was used to keeping the scratch marks on her arms hidden inside her jacket, but there were no sleeves to this gown. She was dressed like Mimic. If only she could crawl up the walls and into the palace's shadows, too.

"The Worm won't want me," she muttered, or thought she did. She might have only meant to speak. Her throat didn't feel enthusiastic about trying.

A familiar pair of clasped hands floated close. Something shiny poked over their wrists, and when the palms opened, they revealed a broad silver circlet that fit across Monique's brow.

"There," said a king's familiar voice. "You should be more comfortable now."

Those same gentle hands stroked Monique's bare shoulders and pressed her down. She reclined across cold stone, the world sweeping out from beneath her body. Steady fingers explored up her gown, where their fingertips traced her inner thigh, stirring a confused hurricane inside her. She reached down to guard private places, but these were familiar fingers and they knew how to tantalize nerves while avoiding scars and months-old aching.

A shadow crossed Monique's bleary world. It had Donna's blue eyes.

Soft weight settled across Monique's prone body, where lips kissed first at the meat of her bicep and then between her shoulder and neck. A shock skittered beneath her skin, and she gasped hard. She reached to feel for Donna's hips, hands, the small of her back, and found Donna's inner thigh, soft and wet and welcoming. An exploring tongue swept lightly along her throat, beneath her jaw, gentle enough to draw tears. If she was stronger, Monique would've twisted around like in their old apartment, where she and Donna used to taste each other until morning.

The tears cleared Monique's eyes. This was no apartment. Glowing fungi offered scant light that climbed stone walls. A balcony hung partway overhead. Higher than that, the ceiling curved into a dome, where slender windows gave glimpses into the room.

Faces filled those windows. Their eyes had watched her nakedness, her scars. They were watching her reunion with Donna.

"They're looking," Monique said between panting breaths. "We can't."

The tongue wouldn't let her go. She gritted her teeth. It would be easier to flow with Donna's touch and pretend a river of ecstasy might wash her away from the Worm's maddening world.

But easy wouldn't save their lives. Monique forced her head up and pushed Donna away. "We have to stop."

Her palms sank into moist, hairless flesh. An enormous wet worm writhed across her legs and chest, its boneless form sagging around her joints. Donna's blue eyes shined from its pink faceless front. A curious tongue prodded Monique's neck.

She screamed and thrashed. No, not this. She wouldn't be this thing's bride.

The haze cleared in full as the weight lifted. "This is no kingly primae nocta," Donna said. "You were my love first. But have it your way."

A dozen hands drew Monique up from cold stone and guided her onto a soft seat. Time thickened into a stone table that reached down the dim throne room, its aged books and silverware having been pushed to either side of where she had reclined moments ago. The table's jagged end stuck out on the far side of the room, undisturbed. Dead men sat in five of the stone seats, their faces covered in silver masks so they couldn't have seen her nakedness, while a sixth seat stood empty.

Monique felt another, larger seat beside her, somehow even emptier, the reserved vacuous place of a god. She had reached the bottom of the throne room and its throne.

At the side of the empty place, and for the last time.

She pressed her feet to the chilly stone floor, started to stand, and then collapsed. Her seat creaked—not stone, but thatched wicker. The Worm's people had dragged this new chair down the elevator, into the throne room, and beside the throne just for her. Lighter, daintier, fit for a bride.

She patted at her head. The silver circlet already felt like a part of her.

Donna paced one side of the table as she buttoned the front of her suit. "We couldn't find your beanie," she said. "But just as well. It wouldn't have looked appropriate for the ceremony."

Young men and women flitted around the bridal chair, once more fiddling with Monique's hair and stirring dishes of mushroom and fish. She didn't recognize their faces, but their hands seemed familiar.

"It was always going to be you, Mon Amour," Donna said. "Even when the Gray Maiden grabbed all those wrong people, I knew you'd find your way. She mixed up the details, only ever fragments of the bride coming home, never the whole of you, but that couldn't stop us, and it couldn't stop the Worm. His will brought you where you belong."

Monique tried to swat hands away from her hair, but her arms felt too heavy. "All those people."

"I take responsibility. I gave too many details or not enough, and she never wanted to come home empty-handed." Donna paced closer. "Living rough? She understood that. Red's a familiar color, but she'd forget where you wore it. I described your features, but her kind probably don't see the distinction, and I didn't want her to grab every trans—well, every woman like you who she came across. Can you imagine, surviving Old Time, only for me to turn her into a bigot? I'd feel so embarrassed."

"Embarrassed?" Monique asked. "Dee, this is murder. Some of those people are dead now. If you keep me, they'll kill me."

Donna paused between the bridal seat and the throne, at last putting her warm body between Monique and the cold clawing of the empty place, the way it should have been in Freedom Tunnel. Yet Monique still felt cold fingers. Donna's presence couldn't keep its grasp at bay.

One of the young women quit fussing with Monique's hair and plucked up a silver fork. Its points slid into a cooked mushroom cap, brown juices sliding down the tine, and brought it to Monique's lips.

She pursed them and turned away, though her needy stomach rumbled.

"I'm not killing you," Donna said. "I'm giving us the gift of a world without hate." She took the fork from the intrusive hand and waved her servants away. A king could do that. She knelt in front of Monique and offered the mushroom again. "Please. I know you're hungry."

Another groan erupted from Monique's stomach. She couldn't fight it anymore. Her lips slid open.

Donna pressed the fork into Monique's mouth and drew it back empty. "This must be preferable to starving in the streets."

Monique grunted. When she finished chewing, she found a cup in her hands. The water came crisp across her tongue and down her throat. She ate sparingly, not wanting to throw it all up after running so close to empty for days. The mushrooms were moist and spongy, the fish tender. To her angry stomach, this was a banquet fit for kings.

Even King Donna.

Monique swallowed one last bite and then shook her head.

Donna relented, placing the fork back on the stone table. Its refection caught briefly in one dead man's silver mask. "That should give you strength for what's to come," she said. "The Worm's never had a bride before. We aren't sure what to expect."

Monique was sure. She'd seen what the song did to Phoebe. "Snap out of it." Monique's voice cracked, going hoarse, but she didn't care. "Please wake up."

"I'm awake." Donna reached over the table and began to part bowls and books from a small blue box. "You act like this isn't me, but I know you better than anyone. I'm the only one who knows how special you are." She placed the box at the head of the table, within arm's reach of Monique—a wrinkled cardboard package of blueberry Pop-Tarts. "You always had the worst taste, Mon Amour. You're still you, and I'm still me."

Donna could preen all she liked, but she was wrong. The underground had eroded her, day by day. While the Worm's people let her keep her wits, they had turned her mind self-destructive. What remained of her had faced choosing her girlfriend or a god, and she'd chosen a god.

"You were always brimming with love," Donna said. She sat against the table's edge and reached for Monique's hair. "Too soft for a world like this. Too special. You deserve better."

Monique clenched her fists at her sides. "There's nothing special about me."

Donna's cheeks blossomed above a wry smirk. "Of course there is. You could've continued pretending to be a son to your parents. You could've given up on me. There were a thousand times you could've made your life easier by doing what everyone else wanted."

Monique looked to her lap. The gown was thin. If she stared long enough, her gaze might pierce its fabric and find her scars. "Doing nothing wouldn't have been easier. Not on the inside."

"That's exactly what I mean. You're a fighter, and you never quit." Donna waved a hand in an arc that passed both bridal seat and throne. "You have this inescapable gravity, perfect for the Bride of the Worm. You'll ensure the Worm's will is done past the physical world, beyond the time we generate by gravity, into the grand role that Earth will take on a cosmic scale. His children will grow inside you, feeding on future what-if's, reflections of Earth from this moment that will never come to be, pathetic Wormless futures. When your children are grown, you'll rain them across land and sea, our eventual inhuman kings."

"I don't even have a fucking uterus!" Monique snapped.

"It doesn't matter. You won't be human anymore. More importantly to him, you have the soul of a mother, caring and resilient." Donna slid her hand from Monique's hair and traced a finger down her jawline. "This fight is your last. You'll be taken into his fold, but that you'll fight? That makes you special."

This wasn't the Donna who once sang across Coney Island or who'd dragged Monique from hospital to church to shelter this past winter, weak and weary, scarred and hating life. King Donna remembered old Donna, but they were not the same. A fundamental switch had flipped.

"You missed Marigold & Cohen, huh?" Monique swatted Donna's hand away. "Mon Amour this, Mon Amour that— you were climbing the ranks, and I dragged you down. Now you've dragged me down, and you're climbing again. Did they hand you a crown on the street, or did they wait until you got here and told them you'd hand me over?"

"I love you. Don't you know that?" Donna looked incredulous. "I never meant to abandon you. I just went for a walk that day, raging over Samuel Reinhart."

Monique's skin felt too tight. "Why?"

"That's the question I asked myself. Why would the world let him do that to you? Why were you even put in that position? Why any of it?" Donna spread her hands to the wall of stars behind the throne. "And the Worm answered. Something wondrous happened for the first time in decades—the Worm chose a new king."

"The Worm changes you," Monique recited. She'd heard that too many times since this began and now it dripped from her own lips.

"He did. And he'll change you, too. Want to know how?" Donna's fresh grin looked eager to tell. "Because we're not wandering the darkness anymore, and that makes us better. You can't stay lost and cynical once you learn there's a purpose to life. I worried you might miss out, but then I realized you'd make the perfect bride. You care, you fight, you love hard and never stop. A king fills each seat once more. The Worm is coming to demand again, and this time he'll have the mother of his children. Soon there won't be people like Doctor Sam to hurt the people I love."

"Because you'll hurt me yourself." Monique tried to stand again. Her legs wobbled. One foot screamed until she fell back into her seat. "If you still love me, drag me out of here. The Worm wants more than my damn kidney, Dee."

"The Worm gives more, too."

"You be the bride then."

Donna scoffed. "I don't have what it takes to be the bride. I have the soul of a king." That was true. Self-righteous, selfish—at Marigold & Cohen, her confidence and ego had been charming. In the Sunless Palace, she was a monster.

Cold fingers tapped down Monique's vertebrae. She glanced past the throne at the wall of stars. The fungi inside its holes seemed to glisten.

"We must be arriving," Donna said, standing from the table. "For us, it's a matter of creeping across time and preparing for his return, but for the Worm, it will have been less than an instant. He's just smashed the continents. Now he's slipping across millions of years to see his work. In a way, he is constant, and time revolves around him."

Monique thought of Corene. "A worm through a wormhole."

"See? You understand." Donna reached for Monique's face. "I would've made you my queen if I could, but the Worm demands, and a world without hate awaits. I'm sorry—"

Monique clamped her teeth down on Donna's hand. A copper taste flooded her mouth.

Donna wrenched back. Teeth marks cut a semi-circle through the meat of her palm, beneath her smallest finger. She smiled as if this proved a point.

Monique spat blood on the floor. "What if there is no he? That cosmic energy screwed up history, but that doesn't make it a god any more than the sun. You're kowtowing to a stellar freak accident. You're killing me for nothing!"

Donna's regal façade slipped to a snarl. "Transcendence, at last, and you shirk it. Do you know why? Because you'll bloom, and you can't handle that. When you lived with your parents, you pretended to be what they wanted for survival. Once they kicked you out, every day was a new struggle. The best you've ever done is survive. You've never thrived."

"I did. With you." Monique felt petulant and hated it, but what choice did she have?

"Not even with me." A gloom fell over Donna's eyes. "It was irresponsible to fall in love with you, Monique. I've had a lot of time to myself in this room to reflect, and I was never really fair to you. I was desperate for love and wanted someone who wouldn't turn her back on me. You had your challenges, but you dogged after me, my loyal sweetheart at half my age. We were never on even footing. Anyone else would've given up long before now, but you tracked me down here yourself. Too young and inexperienced to know better."

Monique gritted her teeth. "I don't quit."

"And look what that's done for you. You're on the verge of starving." Donna's cold shadow crossed the bridal seat. "But I think living on the edge keeps you fighting. You're so used to survival that if you had a loving home and everything you needed, you would lose your mind, tear down your life, and bite the hand that feeds you."

Monique looked to Donna's bloody hand. It wasn't true. She'd been happy when they lived together. But then, her standards for happiness had never been all that high. Her parents had seen to that. Was Donna right? Monique didn't have months in the throne room to contemplate her place in the universe. She had moments, and they were ending.

Donna's eyes focused into a kingly gaze. "Wild Monique, at last your struggle is over. You'll become the vessel of universal future and find peace through your children."

"I don't want to be a mother!" Monique shrieked.

Donna leaned into Monique's face and slammed lips against lips. The kiss brought too much teeth, but Monique didn't shy away. She tasted Donna's blood again. A warm ripple spread through her nerves. She sank into her bridal seat.

Donna tore away before she could catch another bite and turned toward a wall to the throne's right. A slender doorway hid between shadows in the stone. She reached a hesitant hand ahead as if searching for an unseen doorknob.

Monique forced herself to stand. Her foot begged for mercy and the gown tangled around her ankles, but she had to try. "Where are you going?" she asked.

"I've worked the Worm's will. And now—" Donna slipped through the doorway. Shadow covered her black suit and dark hair, and she vanished from the throne room. "Now I've been dismissed."

Bones clattered at Monique's back, drawing her gaze to the table.

The skeletons wriggled. Their hands twitched at their sides, a rattle against stone. One head fell forward, slamming its silver mask against the table. The skull caved in on impact and sent a tremor down the skeleton's spine, shaking loose limbs and ribs. The ribcage collapsed into a crumbling pelvis, and a bowler hat dropped to the floor.

The rest of the silver masks crashed. Down the table, the skeletons crumbled against their seats, spraying bone dust into the air and pearly fragments across the floor. Their clothes crumpled. Whatever force once held the bodies together at last let them fall apart.

They were dismissed.

"No, no, no." Monique darted for the wall's slender doorway. She spun without meaning to, nearly tripping on her gown, and faced the table. She turned around once more, tried another run, and swiveled toward the table again. "That can't be right."

She marched back and forth twenty times, her foot pleading for her to stop. Her legs groaned, every step an effort against gravity, as if she were trying to fly. Blood seeped through her bandage, leaving dark splotches on the floor. When she could hardly walk anymore, she drifted back to the bridal seat and glanced at the throne. This was like trying to step inside the empty place. Anyone who wanted to cross the line would always be dissuaded.

She had not been dismissed.

The rest of the seats now sat empty, every regal hopeful to come before Donna freed of his burden. Monique was alone. Even dead men had more freedom than she did.

Iron doors clanged open and echoed off the dark stone walls. Donna appeared over the balcony railing, her face beaming with pride. This looked more her style, her standing above and Monique below.

Bouchard joined the watchers in the viewing dome windows. His hands remained at his sides. He only conducted ceremonies on the surface, but now they were in the realm of kings and he was just another of the Worm's humble servants. His face said he didn't mind. He was calm and complacent, as Lady might have been had she lived to see this long-awaited moment.

Several more faces joined King Donna on the balcony. Monique recognized Israel and other members of the Worm's choir. The rest had to gather behind them where she couldn't see them. Each wore a crooked line of red dots across their forehead—the constellation of the Worm. Blood seeped in uneven red streams down their faces and necks. All stood naked except Donna. Wrinkled, scarred, pockmarked, insect-bitten, tattooed, pierced, striped with stretchmarks—they were beautiful flesh and blood. They could choose to stop this.

Something glinted in Donna's hand. She pressed a trigger, and Monique's switchblade popped free from its handle.

Monique clenched her teeth. "Don't," she hissed.

The blade's point pressed to one side of Donna's brow and then carved across her forehead. Seven stars for the Worm. She didn't flinch once.

The balcony's heavy doors jostled against their hinges as the Gray Maiden ducked between them. She stopped at

Donna's side. Her talons glistened in the throne room's fungal glow.

"Long ago, in a time now dead, one note changed our world forever," Donna said.

The Gray Maiden wrenched her head back, revealing hints of leathery skin. "OOH!" Her hoot was a foghorn again, harsh and booming.

Monique felt the wall of stars squirm behind her.

"That note began a song in the seer's lone throat," Donna went on. "That first singer summoned our greatest blessing—the Worm. And tonight, the last song stirs through a throng of throats. Where there was one, there are now many. The way will open. We sing the song that pierces the universe and bring the world to its knees."

Donna smiled, that Doctor Sam *this won't hurt a bit* lie of a smile that Monique had seen in Bouchard, too. King Donna then let loose a long, eerie note. It was unsure, unpracticed, but she only sang to get the choir started. Her lips shut as theirs stretched open.

And the world trembled.

15
THE SONG THAT PIERCES THE UNIVERSE

AN OCEAN OF DISSONANT VOICES filled the throne room. They began in the ceremony room's familiar hum, but new layers joined it—a deep bass, arias that climbed and fell like waves, a bright crescendo that brought all voices into momentary harmony.

The notes took on the Gray Maiden's talons and punctured Monique's skin. She covered her ears, but her skull pounded a rhythm of its own. A melodic bridge beckoned her to cross. Her head lolled onto the soft thatched back of the bridal chair.

In her upside-down gaze, shadows crawled across the wall of stars, its surface a starlit puddle that now trembled with waves of sound. She thought of Phoebe, who'd died to a lesser choral cry. Hers would be a gentle whisper to Monique's death, a triumphant anthem of celestial chaos, the Worm's song beautiful and complete.

This wasn't the first time she'd been put in the wrong position and handed the wrong expectations. Her parents used to tell her she would become a man someday, a meaningless word to a child. She'd been ambivalent until she learned that it meant becoming her father or something like him, and then came horror and emptiness.

She once fantasized tragic deaths. Only later did she dare fantasize tragic lives. If she'd known more, she could've found help. Better places, better people to hand her heart than Donna. Other women had stability and support, but Monique never knew how they managed it. There was a lot she didn't know, and now she wouldn't even learn how it felt to grow old.

The choir was going to kill her. Was their song a frequency that bent dimensions or a loving call that summoned a god from the stars? They would either end her life by filling her with unwanted cosmic worm eggs or an interstellar force would pour through a wormhole and tear her to shreds. Maybe the difference was as hair-thin as when Phoebe had been stretched across time and disintegrated. Healing and harm could be a matter of perspective. Monique knew what it felt like to watch; now she'd learn what it felt like to die.

If she did nothing, didn't fight, wouldn't she become a thing the Worm wouldn't want? Nothing special; just Donna's sacrifice.

Monique doubted that. Even if the Worm was more than a non-sentient series of wormholes, he had never shown concern for the character of his bride. He had asked for any daughter from the old kings. It was on the kings to volunteer someone they loved, and only King Donna had stepped up. The Worm didn't care who mothered his children so long as his kings showed supplication.

Monique looked to the jagged end of the table where once sat the seer turned Broken King, a forever screaming skull and torn abdomen, frozen in black glass and stone. The Worm had shown no love for mothers. This moment, this song, would be Monique's only ceremony. Beyond that, she would become the Worm's fertile earth, nothing more.

"Ooh?" A high-pitched cry snuck under the wavering song.

Monique looked to the Gray Maiden, but her songs were too deep. Higher then, near the viewing windows where Monique had first glimpsed this horrible room.

Mimic clutched the ceiling above one window, her talons clinging to its frame, her gown draped against the wall. Her sister-creatures appeared above neighboring windows. The Worm's followers didn't seem to notice; they gazed only at the wall of stars. Mimic and the others stuck to the shadows and descended into the throne room.

Pitiful daughters of the old kings. None were offered to the Worm, but he kept them in his own way. Now they were here to see Monique off, bridesmaids to the Bride of the Worm.

She sat up from the chair. No, he hadn't kept them. They had leaked through from Old Time by accident, his wrath giving a window from their dead time to this one. Even the Worm could make a mistake.

If the daughters had survived, then Monique could, too. She had never meant to do more with her life than keep living and she wasn't going to drop it without a fight. Donna was at least right on that count.

The Gray Maiden turned her head from side to side. "Ooh."

King Donna was too high on victory to notice. Her choir carried on.

"Stop singing," Monique hissed. She grabbed the box of Pop-Tarts off the table and flung it at the balcony. It struck the railing and burst, raining shiny packages over the floor. "Stop it!"

That caught Donna's eye.

Monique grabbed an old book and threw it hard as she could. It tumbled over the balcony railing and landed in front of Israel. If he wavered, she couldn't hear it in the song. She grabbed bowls, cups, spoons, one of the silver masks, still coughing up bits of dry skull, and chucked them, pelting balcony and singer alike.

Mimic reached the floor but clung to the edges of the room. Her sister-creatures kept climbing the walls.

Monique's legs wobbled again, but she grasped the table this time and stood. She could manage this. Mimic reached ahead as if balancing herself, too.

"I'm not alone," Monique whispered.

Soft wind tugged at the hem of her gown and drew her eyes back to the wall of stars. A draft seemed to flow into the dark patches at its edges. There were maybe a dozen holes still glowing with fungal light. The rest had gone dark.

She grabbed the back of the bridal chair and dragged it alongside the table. Mimic pretended to do the same on hunched birdy legs. It was a hard, hobbling journey, but Monique reached the jagged end of the table. She set the chair where the Broken King's throne must once have sat and dropped into it.

Mimic didn't squat beside her. Her head cocked.

"There's room for both of us." Monique scooted to one side of the chair. "Don't leave me alone."

But Mimic wouldn't sit. Something wasn't right. Taking the place of the Broken King wouldn't help. It would only give the Worm another victim.

Donna leaned over the balcony and peered into the darkness. "Who's down there with you?" she asked. She glanced at the Gray Maiden and then into the throne room again. "They can't help you. They aren't even human. Their time is over and ours has come."

Not human? That was fine. Humans hadn't done much good for Monique so far. "Maybe in Pangaea, they thought their time had come," she said. "Look at what the Worm has done to see what he's going to do."

"He gave them kingdoms."

"How did he do that, Dee? What exactly did he give them, a constitution to live by? Sunless Palace blueprints? They had their own culture and language before they ever found him. He gave nothing. They built kingdoms themselves to worship him, and he crushed them."

From the far side of the room, Monique counted maybe eight stars left on the wall. Darkness seeped across where their fellow fungal holes once glowed. An amorphous shape wavered in the spaces between.

Donna patted the balcony railing and crooned another awkward note. "More feeling! Put your hearts into it!" Her choir obeyed.

Monique stood on shaky legs. Two of Mimic's sister-creatures reached the floor and began to skulk the room's perimeter, yet they kept their distance from the shrinking wall of stars and the Worm's brass throne.

Seven stars left on the wall. Its dark edges took on faint light, the wisps of a faraway nebula. The empty place was reaching for it, and for Monique.

She needed to get out. The balcony was full of people. Someone had to be willing to help her. Everyone was convinced Donna would abandon her—even Donna herself believed so—but they could be wrong. Monique needed them to be wrong.

She shoved the bridal chair up against the table and tried to lift it. Her arms could handle it, but her wounded foot groaned beneath the strain. The chair's back struck hard against the table's edge. If she broke it, she'd be throwing away her only boost.

Mimic helped lift the other side. She seemed in the mood to imitate again. Monique wondered if she had been this way in Old Time, always parroting one of her sister-creatures or whichever old king was her parent.

"Ooh," was all she would say.

Monique's foot shrieked bloody murder, but she and Mimic heaved the chair onto the table. Monique climbed after it, Mimic at her side, and they dragged it down the stone surface so that it rested beneath the center of the balcony's lip.

Donna stared down, her expression an emotionless void. Blood had trickled and stained her cheeks, and fresh drops spat down on Monique's face.

She let them dribble as she climbed onto the bridal chair's seat. Soft wicker sagged underfoot, but there wasn't time to be careful. Only four fungal stars remained in their wall, its edges giving way to the distant twinkle of the real thing.

Mimic hunkered at one corner of the table. Her sister-creatures seeped in and out of shadow.

Monique clambered onto the back of the chair, its narrow rim digging into her arches, and leaned against the bottom of the balcony. Her foot's wound popped open, spilling a fresh red glob down the chair's legs. She couldn't keep stable for long. She reached one hand upward.

"Dee, help me," she said, wincing in pain.

Donna was a statue. "Stronger."

Her singers bellowed, and the song became a raging river. Every note tore at Monique's gown, threatening to spill her back onto the table. She groped at the balcony, desperate for a perch to haul herself up. One fingernail pressed hard and snapped off the nail bed, exposing raw flesh to the cool air. Her scream was tiny against the song. Choral voices drowned her out.

"Someone, please." She looked into every eye.

They didn't see her, same as they hadn't seen Phoebe or anyone else they'd sang to pieces. Each either wanted the world that Donna promised or was afraid they'd lose the one they had should the Worm find them wanting; maybe both. Monique's life was a small price to pay.

She kicked off the bridal seat's back and sent it clattering to the floor. There was nothing below now to catch her. One hand grasped the railing, but it was slipping. The other slapped at stone, desperate for a perch.

"Donna, you loved me!" she screeched, reaching for a hand.

But there was no hand to hold. Donna's fingers splayed against the railing. "The Worm is grander than love," she said. The choir thundered around her. "This is where you belong, Mon Amour."

Monique's muscles tugged around her heart. She'd searched for Donna, found her, traveled down here to save her. She didn't deserve this. Donna didn't deserve her.

Monique yanked hard, tearing at her shoulder, and hauled herself up. Her free hand clawed at Donna's face. Overlong nails ripped into skin. Monique was sure it hurt, but still less than Donna's betrayal. She could never bring Donna so low.

"Ooh!" The Gray Maiden swatted one vicious arm along the balcony and knocked Monique aside.

"Don't!" Donna shouted, but she was too late.

Monique twisted half-cocked through the air. The throne room spun. Her lower back crashed against a hard, narrow surface with a sickening snap, and she crumpled between the arms of an open seat.

The world blurred. Blackened. Brightened.

She couldn't pass out. There wasn't time for sleep anymore, and the song was no longer an eerie lullaby. She tried to stand, but her lower body wouldn't unbend. The pain in her foot was gone, replaced by strange static. A harsh ache shot through her shoulders and down one arm.

Donna was speaking. "What do you think you're doing? Get up."

Monique could move her left arm, having fallen on her right side. Donna's blood coated her nails. Her right arm stuck out from beneath her. It twisted wrong at the elbow, and jagged bone now protruded from her forearm. She couldn't move from the icy brass armrest beside it.

Where was she?

"Get up!" Donna shouted.

Monique glanced at the table. Her bridal seat had fallen on its side, one leg having snapped off. Mimic lingered beside it. Behind her, the table stretched to a jagged end, opposite where Monique lay.

This was the head of the table. She had fallen into the Worm's throne.

The empty place.

It wanted her out. She wasn't meant to enter as a solid body, only once the song had torn her apart and fed her to it atom by atom, stretched between tortured afterimages. She dug at the throne's edge with her good hand, but every movement sent ravenous teeth through her nerves. Static filled her spine. She'd have cold fingers on her at any moment, clawing through her thoughts, always present, always needy. She needed to get out.

Yet she remained.

Impossible. The empty place had always dissuaded her. This had to be a mistake.

Mimic approached the table's head and lay on her side, one arm jutting out, acting as Monique's mirror. One mistake faced another.

Even the Worm could make a mistake.

Donna's breath hissed through her teeth. She pointed into the throne room and glared at the Gray Maiden. "Do something! Get her out of there!"

The Gray Maiden glanced over the balcony and then waded through the choir and out the creaking iron doors. Heavy footsteps pounded through unseen corridors.

Mimic's sister-creatures gathered together, three climbing onto the table's head, two hunkering beneath its underside. Their eyes shined within their shrouds. Genuine starlight overwhelmed the wall behind the throne.

Mimic reached from the table. She couldn't penetrate the empty place by force of will, but she seemed to want Monique's hand. Monique tried to reach but couldn't. There were no cold fingers at her back, only through her legs. Her spine was broken.

Mimic nestled her head against the table, her gown draping over its edges. *It's okay*, she seemed to say. Or maybe that was just what Monique wanted to believe.

Donna looked wild now as she leaned over the balcony, her hair unkempt, her eyes alight with angry fire. "Stop singing!" she shouted. "Stop the summoning! It's no longer pure!"

A few members of the choir stuttered and broke their notes, but the rest couldn't stop all at once. Their song seemed to have overtaken them, and their choirmates had to nudge them or press hands over their bloodstained mouths to snuff it out. Even when they'd all stopped, the song's echo rang through the throne room, a genie unwilling to be bottled once more.

The echoes sang from Mimic's throat. She was beyond asking questions, and now belted out one arm of the Worm's universe-piercing melody. Her sister-creatures took up the rest, their throats better-suited than the choir's to bass, arias, and musical power. Nothing changed in the notes' eerie dissonance, and yet when they sang, the song became the most beautiful sound Monique had ever heard. Melody and rhythm flowed inside her, filling her even within the empty place the way a song should.

She lifted her head and glanced through the spires of the Worm's throne at the wall of stars. Distant suns roamed an unknown sky, lost in a wilderness of cold cosmic decay.

Talons scraped at stone as the Gray Maiden squeezed through the throne room doorway where Donna had disappeared once dismissed. "Ooh!" she threatened at the table's cluster, and then turned to Monique. "Ooh!" Her long fingers reached for the throne.

Monique turned again to Mimic and her sister-creatures. They were bridesmaids at the Worm's wedding, but never the bride. Monique wouldn't be the bride either.

The Gray Maiden's talons slid from empty air, repelled by an unrelenting wall. Monique had seen it a hundred times in Freedom Tunnel, felt it beside her in the night, crossed it in Empire Music Hall, in this room. The Gray Maiden reached again, shoulders hunched up, clearly straining, but no force of will could breach the empty place.

Only a mistake.

It had been a vacuous space awaiting its glorious monster, a pure and empty place fit for a god, but it wasn't pure or empty anymore. A Monique-shaped drop of blood now corrupted its perfect ocean of stars. No longer wretched purity, it grew beautifully tainted by mortal body and soul.

The last fungal star vanished from the wall. There was no stone behind it, only freezing blackness that punched into the throne room. It had expected purity. Instead it flowed through the throne, around Monique, into what should have been an empty place, but was now her place. She was flesh and bone becoming the stars; she was a constellation that had pretended it was flesh and bone. Already, she couldn't tell which came first.

Maybe the difference was a matter of perspective. Starlight hadn't meant to journey here, but since when did their intent matter? No one ever asked the stars what they wanted.

Her gaze swept across the vastness of infinity and then focused on the Gray Maiden, Mimic, and their sister-creatures. The throne room folded around them. The Gray Maiden stood dwarfed beneath collapsing shadows, a surviving fragment in an unfair universe. How had she ever seemed so tall? Her final "Ooh!" broadened into a foghorn's scream as cloak and rot and talons sank into dark stone.

The sister-creatures sank behind her, less resistant, finding familiar black glass drinking their hearts and souls. Mimic clasped her hands beneath her head and waited. They were fading musical notes, but their song stuck in Monique's head.

Table, seats, silver masks, and the Worm's brass throne crushed against each other until they became a mashed conglomerate between flattening walls. Stone collapsed across patches of glowing fungi. Dust spilled down Monique's growing shape. She imagined sifting fingers through the debris and learning everything the Sunless Palace had ever seen, but there was no need. This was the end.

The balcony sank beneath her. How had it ever looked so high up? Now Monique reached across its stone railing with ease, where she poured her enormity across the nearest nameless singer. Body and soul snapped beneath her.

One death wasn't nearly enough. She unfurled across Israel in that same moment, and then another boy, and then the rest of the choir. She reached above them for Bouchard and his fellow onlookers, who had praised genocide and cheered death. Now their faces shriveled into leather and their skulls caved into red-white shrapnel. Their bodies flattened and fused to the palace floor until Monique could no longer tell the difference between blood and stone.

King Donna, the last alive, collapsed on hands and knees. "I swear fealty, great Worm! I'm your—" Her throat snatched her voice. Tears and blood streamed down her face. She sank not deeper into the room, but into herself.

She was too pitiful to crush.

Monique turned from her and burrowed up the palace. Had hours passed since she first came to Empire Music Hall or days? She couldn't tell anymore—time was now someone else's problem. The Sunless Palace buckled beneath her, its flower wilting. Someone might escape by crawling through its passages to reach the elevator, but none would worship here again. Graves should be respected, their ghosts left to mourn their lives.

She spilled across the subterranean lake and into the Chamber of Old Time. Shapeless starlight reflected in its black glass. If she still had a face, she didn't want to see it. She folded the chamber against her, close to her heart. Corene lay dead within; Monique took her, too. The King of the Broken Throne with her pilfered womb sank into stone, fading from a world that was never hers.

There. The last precious treasure.

Monique climbed from the underground. The song that was stuck in her head pierced time itself and opened past, present, and future to her. There were other directions, but she wasn't ready to travel them yet. A death called to her.

She sang across years—ten, twenty, fifty, she couldn't tell for certain. They were such small numbers against infinity. She knew only the determined moment she meant to see.

Decades beyond the Sunless Palace's collapse, Donna slept in a white hospital bed at the center of a gleaming room. Wrinkles and pockmarks coated her skin. Dotted scars traced her forehead and three parallel scars cast stripes down one cheek, the remains of an old wound that her decaying mind could no longer remember. Shining machines clicked and beeped to either side of her bed. One monitor traced her frail heartbeat. Plastic tubes fed painkillers into her bloodstream and oxygen into her wheezing lungs.

A much younger woman sat at her bedside. Monique didn't know her, but she had been crying. That was fine. She would not be crying much longer.

Beyond the hospital room's windows, the world burned. Wastelands stretched where forests used to grow, and brackish water flooded once well-traveled neighborhoods. Donna seemed one of the last who would reach old age.

Her heartbeat stuttered. Slowed.

Stopped.

This world held no further purpose. Monique sank deeper through time.

Millennia crumbled into soil around her. She looked ahead to a dying sun, billions of years old, its explosive final fate erasing all traces of Earth and its fellow planets. She remembered Pangaea. Across shadow eons of would-be and never-was, she swam black oceans and forgotten constellations until she found frailty between the stars. It was easier than most anyone would believe, but she thought it made sense.

Most of space was an empty place.

The song that was still caught in her head at last slid out in full force; she began to sing. Notes long unknown to the universe now roared across creation. No mortal creature understood this melody. It burrowed wormlike between dimensions imperceptible to mankind, thinning time and space to a hair, to nothing, the difference between human souls and the black emptiness of space then unknowable even to her.

The song's bridge became physical, the kind she could cross. And she crossed it, first back 175 million years to unmake a mistake, and then ahead to prevent another.

Fields and forests swept beneath her. Beautiful black cities formed curving mountains in every direction, their ornate spires stretching skyward. They were lived-in flowers, and the world grew in lush violet around them. At the center of the supercontinent stood a palace that honored starlight, and inside, the old kings gathered around a table of black glass. The pregnant seer sat at one end. At the head, an empty brass throne awaited a god.

Monique poured into its vacuous space, nothing present to corrupt her, and her absolute will flooded the table. Never mind what she'd been about to demand. She needed no bride. She needed no daughters.

The grateful seer placed a hand over womb. A nearly-formed daughter might have come to be called a tall lady,

Gray Hill, Gray Maiden, names given whether she wanted them or not. Now her mother might name her in her own singing tongue. Someday she might name herself if she pleased.

One of the old kings' daughters mimicked the seer's gesture, hand over middle, and the others crooned amusement.

They were all dismissed. Forever. Let the table crack to pieces as if it had never existed. Let the palace stand derelict until its old purpose was forgotten and its people found it a new one. There would be no more altars to starlight, no kingdoms to honor it. The seer's people might resist such transition after long years of being used to cosmic worship, and the work to change that outlook would be hard and soul-breaking, but the world could do better than a carver.

They would never know their ruin. The sundering of Pangaea was Monique's secret to keep. She sang a song of healing to hush screams from beyond the stars and those, too, were her secret. Every moment of human existence became nothing worse than a bad dream from which the world was finally awake.

On the far side of the bridge over which she had crossed infinities, reality cracked, and time seeped through its fissures.

Years crushed against each other as if jammed into a too-small container, every era united in death. Ancient magma flooded digital mega-cities. Dinosaurs migrated across Utah salt flats alongside woolly mammoths, and a Jersey radio station played all the hits for Paleozoic fish as they first found land inviting, a swan song for time itself. This Earth hardly knew its own face, its beginning and end slamming against each other and then becoming one. In a single unified moment, Donna's dream came true—there was a world without hate.

And then there was no Donna, never had been, never would be. White blinding light overtook the skies, a memory of the Big Bang weaving into a premonition of the sun's supernova. One death undone; a birth unmade to pay for it.

The cosmos shattered into glass shards, and then slivers, and then fading stardust, and a cold, empty nothing surrounded the vicious wound of a murdered universe.

A wormhole for the Worm.

Acknowledgments

Writing requires alone time, but nothing is created in a vacuum, and everything we make is a sum of everything we've experienced and everyone we know.

Working with Samantha Kolesnik has been an absolute dream. Sam has been hands-on with this project at every step, a joy to speak with and to work with, and *The Worm and His Kings* could not have wriggled into a more caring home.

Many thanks go to Karmen Wells for her keen editing, encouraging messages, and attention to detail, and to C.V. Hunt/Squidbar Designs for her haunting cover art. I also want to thank Laurel Hightower for her guidance at many times this year and for always championing me, often by delightful ambush.

There are far too many people to name without knowing I'd miss someone and regret it forever. I have the stellar fortune to have a vast support network of readers, reviewers, and fellow authors. We lift each other up. I have to highlight in special thanks Sara Tantlinger, Lisa Quigley, V. Castro, and Claire Holland for talking me through some monumental tough times and keeping me level when I was crashing through strange days.

I couldn't write what I write, at least not the way I've chosen, if not for every queer author who paved the way ahead of me, and every reader who's cheered the rainbow. We make none of this happen alone.

Lastly and more than anything, thank you to my darling J, who gave this book its earliest and most merciless feedback and her sincere critical eye, and still has time to give all the love in the world. She makes anything possible.

Hailey Piper is the author of *The Possession of Natalie Glasgow*, *An Invitation to Darkness*, and *Benny Rose, the Cannibal King*.

She is a member of the Horror Writers Association, and her short stories appear in *Daily Science Fiction*, *Flash Fiction Online*, *The Arcanist*, *Tales to Terrify*, *Monsters Out of the Closet*, and *Year's Best Hardcore Horror, Volume 5*, among other publications. A trans woman from the haunted woods of New York, she now lives with her wife in Maryland, where together they cast hexes, raise the dead, and summon the elder gods, sometimes all in one night. Find Hailey on Twitter via @HaileyPiperSays or at www.haileypiper.com.

9 780578 779799